Preacher's Mountain

DANIEL PARKER

Copyright © 2021 Daniel Parker

All rights reserved.

ISBN: 978-1-7379033-0-7
Masked Poet Publishing

DEDICATION

To my father and brother,
and all the men who have wandered their way through life,
who work hard at becoming men,
despite the great odds against them.

CONTENTS

Acknowledgments	1
The Holding Pen	9
Levi Johnson	15
Thief in the Night	19
Return to the Jail	25
Lord's Night	27
The Sweet By and By	37
End of Days	41
Jacob	45
The Sons, 1962	51
Preacher, 1962	55
Men of the Times	61
The Pitch	65
Golgotha	67
The Valley	71
Levi, 1968	77
End of Innocence	85
King of Kings, 1975	89
Choice of the Prodigal	95
The Trap	103
Risen	111
Saving The Shepherd	119
Journey Begins	125
Winter's Moon	131

Pontius Returns	147
Fog of Memories	153
Gone But Not Forgotten	163
Closer To Thee	167
Broad Is The Way	169
End of the Road	171
From the Mouth of Babes	173
Up the Mountain	177
Fall of Ahab	181
Revelations	191

ACKNOWLEDGMENTS

This story has taken me much longer than usual to find the appropriate blend of fact and fiction. Sometimes life gets in the way, but a good telling takes time, especially when it is inspired by memories. I had some excellent editorial help in getting to the finish line. Rae Waddell, Robin Stetler, Kelly Hartsfield, Bruce Ballister, and Jack Pittman assisted in making this a much better story than where it began. My family, past and present, continue to be an inspiration to keep writing until something well is written. I've tried to do that here, yet any errors that remain are entirely of my own doing and stubbornness.

THE HOLDING PEN

With darkness setting in on the fenced yard of the jail, a pile of clothes lay in a heap on the snowy ground. The men stripped what remained and shivered in line for their chance to smoke. They waited patiently and silently, bouncing from foot to foot, until the call was made.

"Alright, light em up," the guard barked.

Each took their cigarette from a guard, cupped it, and lit it with the flame offered by the second guard, then hopped and skipped across the frozen turf to an open part of the enclosed yard. They did it willingly for a brisk moment of escape.

There were about twenty of them. They were the forgotten souls of the border area between Kentucky and Tennessee, caught in a county with nothing much to offer except law and order. They were paycheck-to-paycheck types, ramblers, hobos, and odd-jobbers. The kind of men who would suffer for the small gains of life, ten thousand fleeting moments of emptiness in between and in conclusion.

Levi Johnson was different. He'd been in for over a year now, only three years removed from an honorable discharge and a decent upbringing. He was still young compared to most of them, still had a bit of color to him, but Vietnam and a survivor's guilt made him appear more worn than his actual years. His hands shivered as he protected the ember of the cigarette and brought it to his lips.

It was a puff and an exhale in the quiet night air, and they each shook and froze for the elixir of the nicotine. These were the conditions set by the local ramrod of a sheriff named Orville Price. Five minutes of smokes and a few dreams of being somewhere else. It was considered a privilege in his jail, and it was not to be had without some form of payment or pain.

"You wanna smoke while you're with me," Price told the inmates, "there will be payment. One way or the other, any vices you bring here, you'll lose them, or you will earn them."

And that's how Levi Johnson survived jail in an accidental place called Boone, a holdover from a lost era, a place built when humanity was cheap for digging, growing, and dying. It was 1974 when the sheriff's department caught Johnson with a large amount of grass tucked into the undercarriage of an old red Ford.

The sheriff had various arrangements made for such cargo in his county. With proper dues paid and the goods transported for use outside his domain, it was a profitable venture. What he couldn't buck were these lone wolves like Johnson who tried to do things on their own and outside his pay-as-you-go system.

When the sheriff's men first brought Johnson in, the sky had let loose and dropped tornadoes that residents would remember until the day they died. The sheriff was both wet and tired as he trudged into his office and shut the door. He attempted to wipe mud from his boots, and he flung the gathered rain from his brimmed hat. He hung his hat on a hook on the wall, then pulled the slick poncho off with one hand and tossed it to the corner. He lowered himself into a green thick squeaky chair behind the desk.

The sheriff licked a finger out of habit and opened the file in front of him.

"Hmmph. Possession. Expired license. No insurance."

The sheriff gazed up at Levi Johnson, held down firmly in a chair by the officers.

"I don't know who this person is. Looks to me like an out-of-towner. Taking advantage of the weather."

The sheriff picked up his pen.

"Let's add resisting arrest."

"That's bullshit," Levi replied.

The sheriff nodded and the patrol officers took turns on Levi with clubs, fists, and a phone book. The sheriff watched. He liked to observe his men do their work in an orderly rhythm. He had a keen interest in structure and discipline. Levi gasped and grunted with the blows. The sheriff checked his fingernails and clipped one off, then opened a ledger and jotted down a note. He almost missed it when Levi fell to the floor and raised a finger toward a picture on the wall.

"Wait!" Levi yelped.

"Hold it," the sheriff called out, and his men stopped. "Mr. Big Shot here has something else to say."

They yanked Levi from the floor by his shirt and sat him forcibly back into the chair.

"Well?" said the booming voice from behind the desk.

Levi looked up from his seat, his face bleeding, bruised, and swollen, his bottom lip puffed up. He nodded at the poster plastered to the wall, black and white letters, bald head, flat nose, small eyes, round chin, dangerous. *WANTED*.

"I've seen him," Levi said through exhalations. "He was quiet. Never said a word. He's got a..."

Levi tapped a finger on his own neck.

"A cross…right here."

The sheriff gazed at the poster and back to Levi.

"You're sure that was him?" the sheriff asked.

Levi nodded and rolled his head against the pain and spit blood. "Is it worth something? Can you cut me a break here?"

The big man behind the desk paused and observed the younger, as if weighing the audacity of the request. His badge made a reflection from the lone bulb in the room, and he tapped his meaty fingers in a click-click-click pattern.

"That scum has been on my wall for seven years, and suddenly, he appears out of thin air to you? That's what you're trying to tell me?"

Levi turned from the poster, past the sheriff, and gazed momentarily at a framed picture nearby. He thought he recognized a familiarity, someone known from his past, then turned toward the floor.

"Wasn't my kind of people," Levi exclaimed through heavy breaths. "Didn't know who he was, but you don't forget. You keep an eye out. Try and avoid trouble."

The sheriff snickered and Levi spit blood.

"Avoid trouble, huh?" the sheriff jested. "You just figured you'd speak up. Do your lawful duty and all."

The big man peered at Levi for a few more seconds, then thumbed to the second sheet in the file.

"Says here you served in the army. What unit?"

"Third Infantry."

"Third Infantry?"

The sheriff looked up from his papers and paused, then looked over toward the framed photo on his credenza and reminisced.

"How is it we lose good boys over there and a troublemaker like you comes back to stir things up?"

Levi turned his swollen head toward the sheriff and glimpsed again at the soldier in the picture frame. He observed a man-sized boy in uniform with the common killer stare draped in flags and symbols.

"This life isn't fair, I tell you," the sheriff continued. "Too much disorder. Can't tell the good ones from the bad anymore. Things used to be easier. Everyone used to know their place in the pecking order. Do you know your place, son?"

Levi didn't bite and the sheriff cast his gaze back to the papers.

"Petty theft, loitering. Well, I'll be. Maybe I do know you. Is Preacher Johnson your father?"

Levi kept his chin tucked at his chest.

"I haven't seen the Preacher in my county for a spell. Didn't even know he had another son. Life can be a riddle sometimes. A Man of God and Mr. Big Shot here. Appears the apple fell far from the tree. Well, you should've stayed in the army. Had some decency to die over there instead of bringing back trouble. Where's your honor, for God's sake? Now, I've got to deal with the Preacher again. I don't like it."

"You see, I view myself as a bit of a minister, too. I don't spare the rod. I don't need nor desire competition with my ways. I assist the men in my care to find their salvation. I've probably brought more men to God than all the ministers in this area combined. Visitors means questions about how I do things, and I think my ways work. The people in this county have told me so through six elections. Six!"

"Anyways," Levi mustered in reply, "can we work something out? Is that how this works? I give you something, you give me something?"

The sheriff smiled and glanced over at his men, who smiled back.

"What exactly is it you think I can give you?"

"A break? Something. Anything. It wasn't even that much grass."

The big man smiled again and closed the file on the desk. He got up and pulled his frame around the corner until he stood next to Levi. He clapped him hard and quick with one blow and Levi crashed to the floor again in a heap.

"That's for trying to be smart," said the sheriff. "I lost a boy over there. Got him back in a box. And here you are, thinking you're some kind of big shot."

Levi pushed up from the floor, and the sheriff grabbed him by the hair and jerked his head back.

"I don't make deals. I make rules. You break 'em, you get broke."

The sheriff pushed Levi away and turned to his men.

"Take him to a cell. We'll do what the Preacher didn't."

The uniformed men picked Levi Johnson up by his shoulders and drug him out.

LEVI JOHNSON

Levi's incarceration in Boone was an unwanted expectation of the oldest son of a preacher, stuck in a cell at the end of the hall with a stretch of time that had no end. Boone and Sheriff Price were one of those places and circumstances that bred contempt for progress. Men like Levi got caught and stayed locked up until the whims of local authorities were satisfied, or they died and disappeared behind bars.

When Burns the jailer came to get Levi from his cell, Levi knew what it meant. Someone had tried to cross through Boone with a package, a bag, or a brick of weed, and the smell of opportunity by the sheriff was in the air. He made Levi go to work.

The drill was always the same: Burns would open the cell, Levi would exit, he'd wait for Burns to lock the cell back up, then he'd walk with Burns down the middle of the corridor quietly and without question. They'd stop at another locked door, Burns would unlock it, and they would exit that door together.

Levi traded looks with faces along the row of cells. Some were new. Most were old. A couple of the familiar ones were missing, ghosts of the past who did their time and disappeared, or worse. He kept tabs on his own number of days and thought on the several things he'd already missed: an old girlfriend's birthday, hot food, and plenty of cigarettes at his disposal. Time rolled on whether he was there or not.

Burns walked beside Levi until they turned left down a tan linoleum-lined hall. From there, one direction led toward a small countertop area for the public and a place for Burns and the other officers to process paperwork and catch catnaps. The other direction led around the corner to one office; an addition to the building in 1968, part of the getting tough on crime pushed under the Nixon administration. The sheriff took this location and had his own entry and exit to the building.

Burns gave a quick tap with a knuckle on the sheriff's door, opened it, nodded Levi in, and then shut the door and stood guard outside. Sheriff

Price looked up at Levi without smiling, then went back to completing the scribbles in front of him.

The sheriff kept the military tradition with the buzz cut and the shave that went to just above the ears. He was over six feet with nothing left to doubt that taking him down would be a painful proposition. The belt and straps that ran across his uniform hinged his weight in and made it appear that most of the man was lodged in the upper part.

He was a man born for authority. If you got on the sheriff's bad side, and most of him was bad, you usually stayed there until death or departure. He kept a long memory and a short leash. He tended to wear his weapon at all times whether on or off duty. He carried the old-style club that was long, thin, and hard as oak. It had a small bend in it from the time he broke an inmate's back for being uppity. Whenever he moved in the big squeaky chair, the club clanked, and the keys jangled, and the leather groaned under the weight.

He had run the jail for nearly thirty years now and planned on winning a record seventh election before he thought about retiring. He'd gotten a hold of the position after Korea, and held on to it through segregation, civil rights, hippies, and Vietnam. It wasn't that he was any more racist or brighter-bulbed than the other men of his era and vicinity. He was simply a faithful product of the time. When he lost his only son to war, structure and authority were all he had left. With the sheriff, crime was kept low in Boone, order was maintained, and no one ever asked how it was done.

Levi stood at attention and waited for the sheriff. He'd done it so many times, he knew the room like it was his own. The sheriff's office was a cave of ribbons, mementoes, and certificates: Officer of the Year, Appreciation from Big Brothers of Boone, Rotary Club President, Kiwanis Club, the State Troopers Association, an Honorary Discharge from the United States Army, and an American flag from his son's burial. The walls were a living shrine for a distinct species of man.

As is the case with many men who acquire positions of power, the sheriff saw Levi Johnson as a tool to be used and forgotten, and nothing more. Marijuana usage had grown tremendously since the 1960's and since Vietnam in particular, a notion the sheriff took as something the weakest soldiers brought back a taste for. He blamed it on the Viet Cong. He blamed it on a weakness for foreign goods. It was all a conspiracy against real American heroes who needed no vices.

When the sheriff finally turned his attention to Levi, it was in an uncomfortable familial tone.

"Getting awful close to Christmas, Levi," said the sheriff without looking at him. "I don't want you getting jumpy on me and doing something stupid. You get what I'm saying to you?"

"Yes, Sheriff."

"You get any wild ideas of going AWOL, I'll bury you. Do you understand me?"

"Yes, Sheriff."

"Any questions?"

"How many days get knocked off for this?"

The sheriff thought on it and pretended to look at a pad of paper on his desk.

"You know, I only ask that question out of courtesy. Your time of service will be up when I say it is up. Is that clear enough for you?"

"Crystal."

The sheriff pushed across a set of keys, a wallet, and a bag of grass rolled up tight in the shape of a plastic-wrapped brick.

"Just had this come in," said the sheriff. "Shit stinks to high heaven. I guess in your world that makes it quality stuff. You know the drill. Be back before the crack of dawn."

"Sheriff," replied Levi, risking the big man's wrath. "You know, it's the holidays. I don't even know who's around right now, who has money. May take some time."

The sheriff gave a stern look to Levi.

"I know some boys who always have money," the big man replied. "Get it done, then get your ass back here."

Levi knew exactly who the sheriff meant. The Curry brothers. Pot-bellied half-breeds who existed in a state of détente with the sheriff. They kept a nursery of marijuana in and amongst the corn and tobacco fields on the family farm. The sheriff knew what they were doing and allowed them their livelihood, if the product was sold outside the lines of Boone and if they paid their fair share of taxes in cash to the sheriff. When the sheriff needed a little extra income for the holidays, he'd increase patrols along Highway 69. Before long, they'd strike gold with someone moving product, and it was simply a given that the Curry brothers would always be a buyer.

Didn't matter that Levi knew the brothers. Those boys didn't think like regular people. There was nothing to learn of them and no code to go by. They simply existed to stay clear of, especially the older one. Levi looked at the ample amount of weed. The smell was strong and fresh. The only good thing to come from this deal was the bit of extra cash that Levi could pocket and a quick stop at the convenience store.

Levi picked up his keys, his wallet, and the bag. He moved to the sheriff's side door, pushed it open, and hit the cold evening air. When the door shut behind him, the sheriff took his walkie talkie and keyed the microphone.

"K-1-1, do you copy?" the sheriff asked.

"Copy," replied the transmission after a brief pause.

"10-36. Make sure we have a clear path for our boy."

"10-4."

THIEF IN THE NIGHT

The icy wind cut when it crossed the jailhouse parking lot, and Levi picked up the pace to his truck. He was under-dressed for the current frigid degree. His teeth chattered curses with each step. He hurried to the end of the lot where his red and white Ford F100 was kept, knocked the ice from the keyhole, and jiggered the door open.

The frozen seats cracked on contact, and he stepped on the gas pedal several times, then turned the ignition. A few whirs and a bang and the truck started up. Levi searched for a scraper through the detritus on the floorboard. He had a twenty-mile drive to the county line on a dead, cold night. The quicker he left, the more time he might have for a stop or two.

He blew into his hands and urged the truck's heater to work with a couple of slaps on the dash. He glanced out into the parking lot where the sheriff kept his green Chevy truck he called the Hulk. Big wheels, struts, a grill on the front, and searchlights up top. Levi wondered how much his late-night runs had paid for the monster truck.

He didn't like being the sheriff's mule, but he'd done it to himself. He'd gone for a quick transaction to pay some bills. He hadn't taken precautions, hadn't listened to the warnings to stay clear of Boone, and too much sampling of the weed and a bit too many beers made him do stupid things.

With a small area of the windshield scraped clear, Levi shifted the truck into drive and pulled out. Hell, he thought to himself, he didn't even have money to get a cheeseburger or a beer. He'd have to sell the damn weed first to steal a semblance of freedom.

Levi had driven the rural route near the Curry's many times, primarily to go fishing or see a girl or get high. He usually stayed clear of their place, property that had been in the family for years, built on the lost bones of the plantation days. The fields were now planted with green peanuts and rye for the winter. The more lucrative crops had been moved indoors under grow lights until the spring growing season and the tall concealment of corn stalks were available.

The farm was along a stretch of road where any vehicle could be seen from a distance. The place was known as a holler, a lick of land between water and a mountain, so when Levi pulled in between the fields and drove the rutted dirt road, it was no surprise that the oldest of the brothers, Robert Curry, was standing outside waiting for him.

Levi slowed the truck to a stop and rolled the window down. He felt stupid for sticking his hand out the window for a wave, but dealing with the Curry boys meant extra precaution and consideration.

Robert Curry was not exactly a splendid specimen of man. His black hair was thick and matted atop a greasy face and smeared glasses. A gut hung over his jeans, barely concealed by a green jacket with small brown burn holes and a pocket for his pack of Winston cigarettes. His eyes were dark and contained the unsettling element of looking nowhere in particular.

He had no care in the world except for his land and his dope. He liked to drink, and when he did, he was capable of violence that had no logic. Only one dog and one brother stayed close to him for any length of time, and the dog had one eye and the brother had half a brain. The thing about Robert Curry was that he never smiled. He might say something peculiar, or even funny, but he never smiled, and it made anyone else in proximity want to leave his presence quickly.

Robert knew of Levi before they ever met, from words exchanged in places that kept small towns small. There were hardly any lights kept on at the farm, some said because Robert could see better in the dark. Dark was when the farm was busy, with people coming and going and disappearing.

Most of Levi's information came from Richard, the younger Curry brother, who would occasionally wander down to fish from the local bridge, and frequently talked out loud to himself. He was dangerous not from cunning but from currency. He was easily taken advantage of, and it made Robert suspicious of anyone that associated with his brother.

"I'm not stupid," Richard would say. *"You're stupid. And I don't have to stay in my room. Turn the lights off. You're not my daddy. Momma left it to both of us. I know how to do things. I'll show you. Wait and see. You just wait and see."*

"The younger one is retarded," an old girlfriend told Levi. *"He's nice and all, just real slow. Now, Robert? He's the one to watch out for. He gives me the creeps."*

So, Levi kept far away from the Curry brothers. Only through the forced transactions of the sheriff would they cross paths, and Levi tried to keep them quick.

"Levi," Robert said without any note of expression and no handshake, and Levi pulled his hand back in.

"Robert," Levi replied.

Robert paused a few seconds to knock another cigarette from his pack, light it, inhale, and exhale. He offered one to Levi, who took it without the offer to light it.

"This is some bullshit."

Levi was hesitant to ask questions and Robert motioned with his hand.

"Let me see what you got," Robert replied.

Levi cautiously passed the bag of weed to Robert, who looked it over and took a deep smell of it.

"It's not right, Levi," he said, and pushed the glasses back up the rim of his nose. "This is our shit. It has a very distinct aroma from the grow methods we use. The smoke comes out sweet and packs a real satisfying high. People pay well for this and now he is selling it back to us. Our own product. I tell you, it's disrespectful. Someone ought to do something."

Levi was cautious and careful with his words.

"You know how the sheriff is," Levi replied.

"No, tell me, Levi, how is he?"

Levi worked to think fast.

"He's an asshole," Levi replied. "Don't care much for the situation myself. Handed it to me and told me to sell it. Suggested I bring it here."

Robert stared at Levi long enough between puffs until the seconds felt like burns.

"How much?" Robert finally asked.

"Five hundred," Levi answered.

"Shit," Robert answered. "Bad enough I have to buy my own shit back for more than I sell it. That's pouring salt in the wound, Levi. Can't run a business that way. Makes a person think the playing field isn't fair."

Levi kept quiet and pushed in the cigarette lighter beneath the radio as Robert placed the bag on the hood. When the one-eyed dog came closer for a sniff, Robert turned and kicked the poor beast. The dog yelped and scampered away while Robert took a wad of bills from his back pocket. He licked his fingers and counted out the bills. Levi checked the rearview mirror for anything else he should notice.

"How's Richard?" Levi asked nervously to pass the ticking time.

Robert stopped counting and looked at him.

"Why? You wanna talk to him?"

Levi offered. "Just asking. Hadn't seen him in a while and all."

Robert observed Levi before returning to counting the cash. Levi regretted his effort to make small talk.

"Tell me," Robert said, "what do you think the sheriff would do if I just took my shit back? I mean, it is mine. Would he be upset? What if you returned empty-handed? Or, how about this? What if you didn't go back at all?"

The color drained from Levi. He tensed in anticipation.

"The sheriff might think you took the shit and ran," Robert continued, and pushed the glasses back up his nose. "I mean, it's not beyond a potential. You've had to have thought about it. Getting away while you could. Get a fresh start somewhere."

"Not really," Levi replied. "Just want to do my time and get out."

Robert gazed off into the dark with his own crazy thoughts.

"I guess that's plausible."

That was the thing with Robert Curry. He didn't need to come right out and say things, and one couldn't tell what he really meant.

Robert finished counting, folded the bills, and passed them to Levi.

"Would probably cost me more in the long run. Have to think these things through, Levi. Cut your losses sometimes. Just a part of doing business."

Levi nodded at the completion of the deal, pocketed the cash, and shifted to reverse. Before he moved, Robert grabbed his arm.

"I want you to tell the sheriff something for me, Levi," Robert said.

Levi fought his apprehension. He needed to swallow but couldn't.

"Tell him…"

Robert took one last inhale of his cigarette and flicked it into the dark, then let go of Levi's arm and picked up his bag of weed from the hood.

"Tell him…happy holidays."

Robert didn't laugh or smile, and Levi didn't know whether to do either as well. He nodded instead.

The truck rolled back slowly in reverse. Levi didn't want to appear too jumpy. Robert watched as the truck lights faded from him. Levi wiped his brow and switched gears. As soon as he got far enough away, he lit the cigarette with shaking hands, and took a quick glance at the rear-view mirror.

Jee-sus.

Levi was tired of this shit. He took a long drag and pushed the buttons on the radio until he found something familiar to distract his thoughts, then cruised a few miles on the icy highway before the first convenience store came into view. He took $20 from the wad of cash, put gas in the truck, then got a six-pack of beer and a cardboard pizza from under the heat lamps.

The first beer gushed down fast, and Levi crushed the can with a squeeze. The store clerk peered up from behind a crossword puzzle as Levi folded a slice of pizza in half and shoved bites into his mouth. He gazed out from the front of the store at the occasional car that passed by, remembering something his daddy had said many years ago on one of their travels from town to town.

"Only crazy people traveling around at night," the Preacher told the boys, keeping his eyes on the bit of road he could see in the headlights. "There's a reason the sun goes down. The Lord wanted everyone to slow down. Take a load off. Even the Lord knew about the need for rest. It's not natural for a man to be up like this in the dark. Living is done in the light."

The buzz came on quickly from the rest of the beer and Levi tossed the crushed cans into a wastebasket, then added to his bounty with some salted peanuts and two packs of Marlboro reds, one which he hid under the seat and the other which he'd gift to Burns. He knew better than to sneak a pack of contraband in, given the many inmates with fingers amputated by the Sheriff.

"Now, you'll remember," the Sheriff would tell the inmate. "It's my house, my jail. You've got seven more chances to get it right."

Tired of this shit, Levi kept thinking. One thing Robert Curry was right about. Why not just leave? Get across the county line. Take his chances. But he knew what would happen. The sheriff wasn't just law and order. He was a zealot. He'd come for Levi, no matter where he absconded. It was the principle of it all. No man alive would get the better of him in his domain. That's what the sheriff based his existence on. He was the greater man, and now and then, it had to be proven.

RETURN TO THE JAIL

Levi pulled his truck into the jail parking lot, put it in reverse, and backed into the same spot he'd left just a few hours before. He cut the lights, cut the engine, and listened to the wind whistle by. He'd sauced himself enough to be numb to the conditions, numb to caring, and he took his time putting himself back behind the bars.

Jail was a place he'd visited as a kid, when the Preacher would lug bibles and lessons to fill idled hands and brains. The Preacher called such places warehouses for the wayward. To Levi, they were for dead souls. The men always had empty stares, and though respectful to the Preacher, looked for something the Preacher never could give them.

The jail in Boone was first constructed in the 1920s for housing moonshiners. It was a cinder block type on the edge of the county with a long row of cells, a couple of offices, and a tan paint job. It stretched the length of the parking lot with a few windows up toward the roof and a yard surrounded by barbed wire. This evening, the walls were extra gray, frozen with a sheet of dirty ice from the previous night, where the rain came in thick droplets, washed across the region, and froze by the morning.

Down to his right were four police cars lined up like obedient soldiers and waiting for the occasional deputy or mechanic to crank them back to life and scrape them free from the ice. The cars were the 1974 model cruisers, mostly Fords, as the sheriff got a good deal and a kickback from the local dealership.

With the coast clear, Levi got out of the truck, one foot down, then the other, and shut the door behind him. He'd never imagined this situation, but he was in it. His mind wasn't on personal embarrassment or shame to the Preacher. He'd never thought like that, never been a willing partner like his brother. He was more ashamed of having been caught. He was smarter than that. Most people would've run now, yet Levi knew the sheriff wanted him to run. It would be convenient. There were always replacements. He wouldn't make another mistake. He'd do his time and leave the area behind.

Levi stuck the key in the sheriff's side door, opened it, and entered. He shut the door behind himself and made sure no one was present, then deposited the keys and the money in the drawer where the sheriff had told him. Levi stopped and thumbed through the greeting cards on the sheriff's desk, observed the same pictures on the wall and the familiar one on the credenza, then the cabinet with the guns locked away. The sheriff thought so little of Levi, that he was so insignificant a person, it was nothing for the sheriff to leave his office open and the guns in the cabinet.

Standing alone in the dark, in a place he knew he shouldn't be, it was a cruel joke, like candy he couldn't taste. The sheriff was pathological in his methods. These men were malleable. There was nothing solid about them. They'd work their debts to society off by doing his bidding, or he'd be entertained by their dying breath. No one would miss them. No one would ask questions.

Yet Levi was smart enough to recognize the scheme. He'd traveled the area, he'd been in jails, and he'd been a soldier. He knew men like Sheriff Price, and he counted on knowing their weaknesses and when the right opportunity would come.

"Try me," the sheriff told Levi and the others, the few times he walked the cells.

He patted his holster. "My fingers tend to get a little stiff. Doctor tells me it's gout. I think it's a lack of activity. One of you boys can help me out. I've got a marksmanship medal that needs to be honored."

There had never been a successful escape out of the Boone jail, a record the sheriff was immensely proud of and mentioned to inmates on a regular occurrence. Refusal to surrender was the code used in those cases and the sheriff was ready to write it.

Levi knew the sheriff could drop him at any time while he was out of the cell. He'd heard the stories and remembered the missing faces as he moved cautiously through the sheriff's inner door. At the entry to the cells, he knocked two times as instructed until Deputy Burns looked through the square heavy glass window and unlocked the door. Levi entered, and Burns shut the door behind him with a clank, a latch, and a turn of the key. Levi Johnson was back home, and Burns knew enough not to record the entry for the sheriff's morning report. Levi knew enough to bide his time.

LORD'S NIGHT

The cold days of December added no comfort to the inmates. The men spent most of their time under blankets, itching for a smoke and distracting themselves with solitaire, reading a weathered and brown paperback, or craning their necks to watch the one television that hung at the end of the walk. With only three stations available, the choices were limited to Sesame Street and Shakespeare just as much as Kojak or Baretta. It didn't matter. It was noise for the times they were forbidden to talk, so they watched it anyway.

Sheriff Price was in early and usually gone early. That's the only way they ever caught a break. When the sheriff was not on the premises, a jailbird might entice Burns or another jailer to let them converse in whispers or turn the television to a football game. It was almost always sports or cops. Wednesday night was the one night they begged for reprieve to watch a new show called Charlie's Angels.

"Why's the television there if we can't watch it?" an inmate quizzed the jailer on duty.

It was Burns, and he kept walking when he spoke.

"No talking," Burns barked. "You know the rules."

"Best not to ask questions you don't know the answer to," answered another inmate from a different cell. "You'll mess things up for the rest of us."

"I know why," offered a different inmate. "So the sheriff can show you who's the boss. He knows you want it. He gets off on that."

Burns stopped and looked at the voice. He knew before he looked that it was Levi Johnson who supplied the answer.

"Keep opinions like that to yourself," Burns told him, then spoke louder for the rest of them. "Loose lips sink ships. You cause me trouble, I'll cause you double."

"You know what I mean, Burns."

"Doesn't matter if I do or don't. You're talking a little too familiar for my liking, so shut it up."

Burns continued on his way. He was the zookeeper, the full-time jailer, with space for a cot in his office should he need it. He was a thin man in his late-50's, wrinkled by time and cigarettes and service tattoos. He kept his pride in his appearance, something military service had instilled in him. The army offered routine and livelihood, so Burns gave them twenty years for the pension that was left after a divorce. Being the jailer was a second career. In many ways, it was an extension of the army, with men herding men and the barking of orders.

Burns kept his uniform starched to perfection out of habit, and he displayed the crisp discipline and order of a man that accepted order as his occupation. His only vices were the Lucky Strike he kept lit between his thumb and forefinger, and black coffee he drank, even if it was a day old, from the cup with the faded 1st Infantry insignia.

Burns avoided small talk with inmates. He knew that Levi Johnson was right. Something about the sheriff was bent, but it wasn't for Burns or any of the inmates to talk about, especially when the sheriff was still on the premises. That was dangerous. Burns finished his walk, opened, and exited the cell block, and locked the door behind him. He looked at his watch and wrote the time down on a clipboard hanging on the wall. As he did, he glanced toward the parking lot and saw a lone figure moving slowly, swaying from side to side, making his way to the entrance.

"Shit," Burns whispered to himself.

It was the Preacher, making his way across the slick pavement, after visiting hours and on the wrong day, holding a bible and a tray. The Preacher had been bringing communion to the jail too many times to count since Levi Johnson had taken up residence. It was too much for the sheriff, who used all his authority to make jail the house of redemption he thought it should be.

Burns heard the sheriff's side door open as he watched the Preacher shuffle across the frozen parking lot in his dark long coat and his thick felt hat.

"Look at this here," the sheriff said, exiting his office and nodding toward the parking lot.

It was the weekend, and the sheriff allowed visitors only on Wednesdays, during a two-hour window, and that was it. If one of these lowlifes wanted to see a mother, wife, or girlfriend, then suffering from not seeing them would hasten their good behavior until release. No one had questioned his authority over such things until the Preacher started showing up.

"What does he think he's accomplishing?" the sheriff asked.

Burns shrugged his shoulders before offering a reply. "Trying to make a difference, I suppose."

"A pain in my ass," the sheriff muttered. "Mr. Big Shot back there has caused me more trouble than he's worth. Might have to do something about that."

When the Preacher arrived at the front door, Burns unlocked it and let him in. The Preacher braced against the wall and dutifully knocked his shoes off and breathed a heavy sigh of relief. The sheriff strolled up closer.

"Isn't getting any warmer, that's for sure," the Preacher said with a smile, balancing his bible and his communion tray.

"Then why don't you stay home, Preacher?" the sheriff replied. "You know when visiting hours are. These men don't need any of what you're selling anyway."

"Quite the contrary, Sheriff," the Preacher replied. "These boys need as much of the Good News as they can get."

"That may fly elsewhere, but not here. What they need is affliction. The hard end of the stick. As much as they can take. Then they can leave and receive whatever belief they want."

The Preacher glanced between the two men. Burns looked away, searching for a quick end to the discomfort of the situation.

"Vengeance is the Lord's," the Preacher replied.

"Is that so?" the sheriff said. "What's your boy doing in here anyway? Did he not get the message? Cause too much trouble at home? Ship him off to the military to fix him?"

The Preacher held the communion tray tight against his bible with his small, gloved hand to keep it from shaking. He looked back at the sheriff with a tinge of righteous defiance.

"All have fallen short of the glory of God, Sheriff," the Preacher replied, "even you. And there will be no rank or uniform when the time comes. We shall all be judged, even by those things we didn't do. Now, I don't know a jail in the area that doesn't allow a man imprisoned to take communion on the Lord's Day. So, unless you have anything more, I will suggest you let me do my job, as it does not interfere with you doing yours."

The sheriff looked the Preacher up and down. He didn't like competition, didn't like being talked back to, and he didn't like the threat of a bunch of Jesus freaks protesting at the jail. While he had the men, they had only one religion, and that was to do as they were told. He'd get them to Jesus faster than any minister would, but he didn't want church troubles getting stirred up either.

"Make it quick," the sheriff said to the Preacher.

"Right this way, Preacher," Burns replied and led the old man down the hallway and toward the cells. The sheriff watched them go with a look of disdain, then turned back to his office.

Burns unlocked the heavy door with a turn of the thick key, motioned the Preacher through, and locked it behind them.

"Like he said, Preacher," mumbled Burns, "Better make this one quick."

The Preacher nodded he understood and shuffled away from Burns. He passed rows of cells. The men inside stared blankly back at him. In this cell, two black men, each bundled in gray blankets, wrapped tight against the cold. In this one, an old man, face red from drink, with the bulbous nose of liquor intoxication. Unkempt men. Disposable men.

The Preacher had seen many such faces over the years. It was still a shock to him to see the face of his own son behind bars. He would never get used to it. He'd given it up to God as one of the many trials and tribulations like Paul and the apostles dealt with. He could go no deeper than that.

In the early going, the other son, Jacob, would drive his father to the jailhouse, dutiful and honor bound. The Preacher would pray, and Levi would take the communion through the bars, then he'd ask for smokes and money and that would end in cursing between the brothers. The embarrassment of it, the gall of his brother; it was too much for Jacob to witness. When Jacob started his own family, he left Levi and his troubles behind. The Preacher aged ever more quickly, but he kept going on his own, twice a week. Despite Jacob's call for his father to let his brother go, the Preacher kept it up, and he kept praying for a miracle to sort out the wayward son.

"We ask these things in Jesus' name, amen," prayed the Preacher.

Levi slipped his hand through the bars and took a small glass cylinder full of grape juice out of the tray and sipped it empty.

"How about one for me, Preacher?" asked an old man, baked from too many times passed out under a blazing sun.

"Shut up and leave em in peace," another inmate hissed at him.

The Preacher observed the old man and held the tray of small cups and beckoned him to take one, which the man arose and accepted through his own bars with a short silent prayer. He threw the juice back and then slipped the empty cup back into the tray.

"Momma tried to tell me," he said to the Preacher. "She yelled hell damnation and some choice words. But here I am anyway."

The man cast his eyes down in shame and retreated to his bunk.

"It's never too late for the Lord," the Preacher called out to him, but the man didn't reply. The Preacher turned his attention back to his son.

"You been staying out of trouble?" he asked.

"It's jail, pops," Levi replied in a lowered voice. "I told you to stop coming out here. It's not safe."

"Not safe? You're in jail."

Levi shook his head at his father. "You don't understand. Did you at least bring me any smokes?"

"Slipped my mind," offered the Preacher, a bit of a white lie from even the best of men.

"How many times I have to ask you. If you're going to come out here, can you at least bring me something I can use?"

The Preacher looked at his son with narrowed eyes and raised his bible.

"This is all you need, son. Been trying to tell you that since the day you were born. I've visited many men in jail. You wouldn't know they were murderers and thieves. There are things in this world we cannot comprehend. It is the great mystery, son. The Lord moved in mysterious ways, especially with sons. There were Abraham and Isaac, and David and Absalom, Eli and his two sons. And of course, you know the story of the prodigal son, the one who would return."

"Aw, Jesus, pops—"

"You have a purpose, Levi, but it's not in here. It's going to be something more, something bigger. You wait and see. Have faith, son. Have faith."

"God, I've had enough of this. I don't need a lesson. Don't need your prayers."

Levi took a few steps back in his cell, then returned to the bars.

"You have no idea of the things I've dealt with. The places I've been. Some of the shit I've seen. So, just stop with the preaching. I'm worn out with it."

The Preacher took it in. He'd followed the Lord's will in raising the boys, but Levi's words piled up stones. Was there something he'd missed with Levi as a boy? Something left undone? Even Jacob had gone his own path. He had failed as a father. No, he couldn't think like that. Doubt was the devil's product. His sons were men now, not puppets. They'd make their own way, their own choices with God.

Levi looked toward the concrete floor, then back to his dad. It wasn't worth sharing. There was nothing the old man could do, so Levi would continue to spare him any details of his life and thoughts.

"Don't come anymore, pops," he said with a sigh. "You're just going to cause trouble."

Levi climbed up to his bunk and lay down. It added to the long silence between them. The old man appeared to be used to these endings and carefully closed the tray without spilling the contents.

Levi looked agitated as the Preacher turned to leave. He was just about to say something when the old man called back to him. "Lord willing, I'll be back on Wednesday."

Levi shook his head at the stubbornness of the old man. The Preacher made his way down the hall, knocked on the door, and was let out by Burns.

"Looks like it'll be a white Christmas this year," Burns said to the Preacher, unusual small talk as he locked the heavy door behind them.

"Seems that way. Lord willing. How are you, Burns? Are you doing well?"

"No complaints, Preacher. Any day above ground's a good day."

The Preacher paused and looked around.

"Tell me the truth, Burns. How's he doing in here?"

"Oh, I reckon he's fine, Preacher," replied Burns. "No problems."

The Preacher looked for the truth in Burn's eyes and nodded in agreement.

"I still don't understand all the legalities. Figured he'd be out by now."

Burns nodded without adding any words.

"I was hoping he might be out by Christmas," the Preacher continued.

"Reckon I don't know, Preacher," replied Burns. "You might check with the county court on that."

The Preacher nodded again and looked at the floor. Burns hated these situations of being asked about something he had no control over, but also because he knew more than he should. He respected the Preacher, respected the pride of the father, and he kept things positive for his regard.

"I'm sure he'll be out soon enough," Burns added. "You better get a move on before the weather gets any worse."

The Preacher gave a quick nod and set the tray and his bible down on a long ledge under the windows. He took out a beat-up brown leather wallet with more bits of paper than money. He slipped out a five-dollar bill, the only one in his wallet, and handed it to Burns.

"Put it in the pot for Levi, would you?" Preacher asked Burns.

Burns glanced to ensure the sheriff was away and occupied, then took the cash.

"Something is not right here, Burns," the Preacher added. "It's not right. Every man must be under a law. Either the law of the land, or God's law."

Burns nodded his agreement to cool the old man down.

"God opposes the proud and gives grace to the humble," the Preacher muttered.

It wasn't the first time the Preacher questioned the sheriff's rules. Burns admired the Preacher, even if he thought his coming and going was a waste of time on Levi.

"I'll get it to him," Burns added, "but do us all a favor. Come during the normal visiting hours."

The Preacher shook his head and tugged his black felt hat into place, then picked up his items.

"You have any plans for the holidays?" he asked Burns.

"Same as always."

Burns twirled a finger in the air.

"Right here. Today, tomorrow, and the next."

"No rest for the weary, huh?" the Preacher replied.

"Something like that."

The Preacher nodded his appreciation. "Well, all the same, Merry Christmas to you."

"Same to you, Preacher."

Burns opened and held the door for the Preacher.

"Thank you."

"Sure thing, Preacher."

The Preacher stepped into the cold. Burns watched the old man wobble across the frozen parking lot until he got to the station wagon. Both the vehicle and the preacher were rusted and faded with time, and Burns glanced from the parking lot up toward the inky dark sky and the brilliant white flakes that fell from nowhere. The muffler beat the wagon to life, and Burns watched through the glass as the Preacher spun the wheel and maneuvered the brown beast from the parking lot.

Burns didn't like secrets, especially with a man of God. It troubled him. He wished he could level with the Preacher. Let him know about Levi's predicament. Get him the hell out of there while he could. But it wouldn't solve anything. It wouldn't end anything. What the sheriff kept Levi busy with, none of it would be good for the old man to know. Probably would kill him. Duty overruled Burn's sense of right and wrong and told him to look the other way. Keep his mouth shut and keep his job.

THE SWEET BY AND BY

The Preacher turned the wipers up and gripped the wheel as he followed the road away from the jail. He reached his hand out to adjust the rear-view mirror and was glad he had his rabbit fur gloves on. It was cold in his bones, and he could still see his breath in the wagon. He fiddled with the knobs for the heat while he kept an eye on the road.

The sensation in his chest was something new, but he assumed it was the common cold he'd recently gotten over. Nothing out of the ordinary. The coughing had left a bit of strain, and he was sore and achy, but nothing that a change of weather and a little sun wouldn't take away in a few weeks. He still had lots of work to do. There was no retirement from doing the Lord's work.

The Preacher had a list of people to see. Brothers, sisters, cousins of cousins, all would love a visit during the holidays. The old timers would call up and ask the Preacher to visit so-and-so since they were too far up in age to travel, or the weather was bad, or a jail would only allow a minister or next of kin, and the Preacher would try and do it all. He'd take the communion tray to an ill sister or brother shut in and even take the dog outside while he was there. Brother Jean was the one who hand carved the wooden pew up front in the little Macon church, and he was down in the back and wanted someone to pray with him. Sister Mabel was the one who'd brought him chocolate pie now and then and she laughed sweetly when the Preacher told her it was so good, he felt he'd needed to take his shoes off to enter holy ground. Sister Mabel's eyesight was getting worse now, and it was hard to drive at night, and could he bring communion now and then? Yes, all of God's people needed to be looked after, especially when stuck at home or dispersed to the beds in the regional hospital or stuck behind bars. For many of them, it might be a last chance to get right with God.

The Preacher always did his duty at the regional hospital. There was always someone to visit or who didn't mind a stranger stopping by to pray. The apostles had dealt with worse, he told himself. He'd return to see his son. He'd visit the sick. He'd comfort the afflicted. If the sheriff or anyone tried to stop him, it was in God's hands.

"Vengeance is mine, sayeth the Lord," the Preacher muttered out loud.

In the distance, the Preacher could see the blue lights and signs of the regional hospital and the red and white Christmas decorations that outlined the large square-blocked building. He was thankful for these opportunities. He liked to feel needed, and he was long aware of living with the unspoken rules. A minister could ill afford a son in jail, and he could not keep his hands from being idle, his mind from iniquities, with no wife at home.

He turned the wheel to the right and pulled up under the entrance to the hospital. The motor coughed to an end, and the Preacher paused to admire the various twinkling lights and how the snow illuminated with great shafts of color. There was a beauty to it, a peacefulness in the fleeting winds of life. He got out, one foot before the other, stiff, and used the door to pull himself up and take a few breaths.

"Sir," a guard at the door hollered out.

The Preacher turned toward the voice. The rotund guard stepped out of the entrance and toward the Preacher. "Sir, you can't park your car here. Only for emergencies."

"Oh, I won't be long," the Preacher replied. "Just a quick stop to see a sister."

"I'm sorry, sir. Them are the rules. There's plenty of parking in the parking lot. I gotta keep this area open."

The Preacher gazed over at the parking lot, then nodded he understood. The guard returned inside, and the Preacher got back in the car, lowering himself down and pulling the heavy door shut. He watched his breath dissipate in the cold air and got the motor started up after a few seconds. He dropped the wagon into gear and crept the vehicle up about a hundred feet and around to the parking lot.

The snow smashed under the rolling tires and the Preacher was thinking about the third floor when he parked, and whether the elevator would work, and the sister's name was Mabel, or was it Ruth? Sometimes he'd forget the name of who he was visiting, and just call them sister or brother. This sister was the one that baked the chocolate pie. That part he remembered.

He turned the wagon off again, grabbed his bible, and moved himself up and out, then closed the door. He pulled his coat tighter against the wind and the bursts of snow and moved along the wagon. His breathing labored, and he thought he'd sit for a moment, just a moment, to catch his breath and enjoy the lights a bit more.

He took a place on the rusty chrome bumper and put his hands on his knees with the bible held tight. He turned his eyes toward the sky and admired the heavens. Didn't matter how old he was or even where he was. It was always fine to take a moment and feel the breath of God on one's face. The snow hit his eyelids and cheeks and he breathed in the crisp, cool air.

He thought on the boys when they were babes and the young wife who promised to have and to hold him through sickness and health until the cancer got her and he couldn't tell her the truth about her illness until she was gone. What a trial. He'd nearly lost his faith over it.

He peered down and watched the snow gather on the old leather shoes polished up good that morning. Something strange now, he knew it had been building since back at the jail. But here it was, no mistake. Something had his chest in a grip as sure as the Hand of God. He blinked at the knowledge, knew it was time. Knew he'd been called and was thankful. He slowly leaned forward, just a bit at a time, until the bible slipped from his hands, and he tumbled to the ground. His dark felt hat rolled on the brim and came to rest upside down. The Preacher didn't move, and the snow gathered into the creases of his coat and wisps of gray hair.

END OF DAYS

The snow blanketed Boone for three days straight without a rest. Local schools closed early for Christmas break and festivities began in haste after the roads were salted. It was just this side of dawn when Levi staggered from his truck and across the parking lot, leaving deep tracks in the accumulated snow. The sheriff had forced him out on the road, given the amount of contraband going around for holiday festivities. The big man's deputies had snagged weed, moonshine, black market cigarettes, and even a few gift-wrapped presents stolen from an orphanage. The presents were returned, but he wanted the rest sold and re-distributed before morning light.

Levi crossed to another county and made a grand for the sheriff. With most of it in his pocket (a few bucks to quickly consumed beer, whiskey, and cigs), he made his way to the side entrance, fumbled with the keys, and opened the door. He was lit, but had done these deals enough times that it was rote; enter as quiet as a church mouse, put all the keys and the money in the top right-hand drawer, leave out the other door, walk straight to the holding cells, knock, and wait to be let in.

Levi slid the drawer open and made his deposit. How many times had he done this now? Forty times? Fifty? He closed it and turned his attention to the safe parked up under the drawer. He'd seen the sheriff open it so many times, he had a good idea of the combination, and his goal was to learn that combination. Just in case, and for shits and grins. There was time to try a new set. Levi listened for noises then took a quick glance at the doors.

He bent down to the safe and twisted the knob. The first click was a 38, then he spun it back to a 35, and the last number he spun the dial to a 30. He pulled on the handle, but it didn't budget. He was about to try another set of turns when a clank and footsteps brought him back to his senses. He pushed away quickly from the safe and exited through the interior door.

Burns was on duty as usual. Levi knocked at the entry to the cellblock. Burns eyed him through the glass, turned a key, and let him in.

"Long night," Levi said.

"Don't care, and don't want any details. Let's go."

"Damn Burns, don't you ever sleep?"

"Got no time for sleep."

Burns shut and locked the heavy door and walked Levi past the cells. Burns never asked Levi questions, and never offered conversation. They walked together, the clap of their steps in unison, past the sleeping inmates. Burns caught a whiff of the alcohol on Levi, but he kept quiet. Leave things well enough alone. With a twist of a key, Burns opened the cell at the end of the hall and Levi walked in.

"Goodnight, Burns," Levi offered quietly.

Burns offered a look and nothing else. He didn't like these extracurricular activities, and he locked Levi in, turned away, and left. Levi listened as the steps faded, the clank of another key turned, the big door pulled open, and then clattered shut.

Bologna and bread. It was still on Levi's bunk, waiting for him. He pushed it out of the way and pulled himself up. What day was it? It felt like a Wednesday. Or was it Sunday? He'd momentarily forgotten. Usually, the Preacher would have brought communion on Wednesdays and Sundays, but communion hadn't come. He thought more on it, then turned toward the wall and adjusted the small hard pillow.

"Not healthy for you to be here," the Preacher had once told him. "Locked away in a cage. Men guarding men. Waiting for their animal natures to recede. Better to put a man to work. Let them live and sleep outdoors. Let them see the sky and the stars. Nature will assist their true Christian identities to shine forth."

Or something like that, Levi thought to himself. He remembered bits and pieces of the Preacher's messages. It was a thousand services and tent revivals and gas stations run together. The chill in the nighttime air forced inmates to curl up tight and entomb themselves under the issued blankets. One good outcome of being the sheriff's errand boy were the few beers and cigarettes that made getting to sleep a little easier. He was content with the fifth of whiskey he'd imbibed before returning. He wrapped the blanket over his head and kept a small breathing hole for the cold air, then fell into a deep alcohol-induced sleep.

Levi dreamed in chalky shades of gray; backseats, rolled down windows, and sweaty dark vinyl. Air that smelled like leaded gasoline and the tang of dust with a bit of old lady perfume. The memories were brief images of places mixed up together, a cocktail of when's and where's emerging into a fountain of faces. He heard the Preacher's words, imploring and pleading for salvation before it was too late, until the images faded into the deep, dark jungle of lost souls.

JACOB

The two chairs in the waiting room sported vinyl covers that had been there long enough for ridges to form in the seats. The brown sofa and brown lamp were waxed tight to the floor. There was a faint glow from the talking heads on the television console as they debated the recent win of the former Georgia Governor Jimmy Carter over President Gerald Ford.

Down the hallway, past the nurse's station, past a row of patient rooms, was Room 301. The clicks and beeps from the medical equipment caused Jacob to stir in his sleep. He was sweaty and pasted to his chair while the Preacher lay ashen on the bed. An IV hung on one side and a ventilator helped push the air from the other. The monitor kept a slow, steady beat as death waited impatiently for the old man to expire.

A nurse entered the room, her uniform still fresh and starched for her night shift. She checked the Preacher's vitals, then stood close to Jacob so she could nudge him awake. When he jerked, she spoke softly to him.

"It's way past visiting hours," she told him.

Jake got his bearings and nodded he understood.

"Listen," she said to him. "I've seen this a few times now. His spirit is strong, but his body is weak. If you have anyone that wants to see him, go home and make some calls. Often, they hang on until they can say goodbye to a certain someone."

Jake searched her face, more of a fight against the obvious. The nurse looked back toward the open door, then toward the patient, and back to Jake.

"You think on it, but don't wait too long."

Jake turned toward his father as the nurse left the room. He was in that familiar role again. While the Preacher yearned for the prodigal son to return, it was Jake who showed up. He carefully pushed the rolling table out of the way, the one with the vase of flowers and the old man's bible with the beaten black leather flap. He bent close to talk to the old man.

"Dad?" he called.

The old man didn't stir, and Jake looked close at the face he'd seen his entire life. He tried to consider the moment when time had caught up with the Preacher, the once vibrant man who had packed them into wagon on multiple journeys to go out and spread the gospel, who made peanut butter and jelly sandwiches with white Wonder bread, and played baseball with a left-handed swing and an old glove with any of the kids in the towns they stopped in. When exactly had this man started to shrink and wrinkle? When had the dark, curly hair his father carefully combed begun the march toward gray and disappearance? The cheeks that were once full and rosy and the voice that sung almost any song from the hymnal book by memory were now sunken and empty. How time weathered the old man away.

The towns and hamlets they'd journeyed through were equally dying. The one-stop train towns with the family farms that fought to survive against the company farms, the main streets of the small towns that emptied when the big box stores set up out along the county lines. The local stores, banks, and grocers were slowly boarded up. The people stopped coming to the tent revivals.

"I've done the best I could," the Preacher told the boys, *"but the Word has a new competition. These people have traded in their roots and their neighbors for fancy little trinkets, television, and mountains of debt!"*

Jake repeated the name he'd called a thousand times as a little boy.

"Dad?"

The Preacher finally stirred, and his eyes fluttered and opened to a peek. He smiled slightly upon seeing Jake and tried to speak but coughed instead. Jake turned away for a moment because he felt the swelling tears in his own eyes. He did not want his father to see him cry. He thought of something else to clear his mind and he turned back to his father with the drink and straw.

The Preacher worked a sip of water down and looked again at his youngest son.

"Woo-wee," his father said in almost a whisper. He put his hand out and Jake took it.

The old man tried to speak again but couldn't get the word out. Jake squeezed his hand and bent down closer to his father.

"Hospital?" the Preacher asked.

"Yeah. You've been here about five days. Said you had a heart attack."

The old man closed his eyes and paused, then opened them again.

"Levi?" he said.

Jake looked at him. His father looked back. Despite Jake's frustrations with his brother, he understood. The Preacher was dying and just wanted to see both his boys.

"Still in jail," Jake replied.

The Preacher slowly closed his eyes with a slight upturn of the lips. Running after his brother was a job that Jake never wanted, but he felt compelled to do it. He hadn't asked to be his brother's keeper. It just came with the territory.

Jake turned to leave when his father pulled on his hand.

"Take me home," the Preacher whispered to him. "I'm dying. I can feel it in my bones. Take me home."

"How, Dad?" Jake asked. "I don't—"

"Home," the old man said feebly. "Take me to the mountain."

Jake reflected on the request. Preacher's mountain home was nearly five hours away. Jake motioned he understood, and the old man released his hand and closed his eyes again. The mountain was the land of fables for the boys. All the people the Preacher told stories of, like the favored uncle they'd never known, the grandparents who'd only had a couple of years with two young boys, the mother who had come and gone with illness so quickly that the Preacher never spoke of it.

Jake left his father's side and went to the empty nurse station. He fidgeted with his thoughts and noticed the nurse talking with a doctor down the other end of the hallway. When she noticed Jacob, she nodded the doctor toward him.

"Mister Johnson?" the doctor said, as he approached. "I am Doctor Noel. I understand the nurse talked to you about your father's condition?"

"He wants me to take him home," Jake replied. "I'll move him out of here as soon as I can make the arrangements."

The doctor appeared unprepared for the statement and paused before giving a response.

"Mr. Johnson, possibly the nurse didn't explain. Your father is in a very weakened state. Moving him would… well frankly, it would kill him. You keep him here, we can make him comfortable, maybe even prolong his time with you a bit."

"Please. Can you just get him something? Anything that'll dull the pain while I move him?"

Jake glanced back toward his father's room.

"He doesn't want to die here. I don't want him to die here."

Jake tried to figure out what more to say. The doctor didn't want to be in this position any more than Jake and hesitated before he moved in closer and patted Jake on the arm.

"Unfortunately, with your father's congestive heart failure and his advanced age, he is in his last days, probably his last hours. Bring your family here. It will be much easier for him."

"We'll keep him comfortable," the doctor expressed as he turned and left. The doctor glanced toward the nurse, who looked away from having eavesdropped on the conversation.

Jake watched the doctor go. He looked down the hall again, at the clock on the wall, at the weather outside, then returned to the Preacher's room and observed the monitors that whirred and beeped while they stood guard around his father.

All the time together, the miles up and down the hills and highways competed for Jake's thoughts on what to do. The Preacher was asleep again, off in his own dreams of the past. Jake weighed the words of the doctor against the wishes of his father. The old man was in the hands of God now. It was more about where he wanted to die.

Jake left the room and returned to the nurse's station.

"Can I use the phone?" he asked the nurse.

She moved to her station and picked up the phone and put it on the counter.

"Dial 9 to get out," she offered, with a look of understanding.

THE SONS, 1962

The parking lot was full outside the IGA, an occasion only seen during the Veteran's Day Parade, Thanksgiving, or Sundays after church. The one exception was a campaign stop three years back by President Eisenhower, when a fish fry and Ike brought more fish and more townspeople than the space could handle.

In this instance, it was midweek of summer 1962 and an extra warm evening. The small-town people looked forward to distraction from the heat and the threat of communists, so much so that they came out to sit under a tent, swat flies, fan the air, and hear the man they all called Preacher.

"Brothers and sisters," he bellowed, "if you feel you need prayers, if you want forgiveness of your sins, if you wish to be baptized into the Body of Christ, please come forward while we stand and sing."

They all rose from the rickety metal and wooden chairs to sing an old Lowery tune they all knew.

"Shall we gather at the river?
The beautiful, beautiful river.
Gather with the saints at the river,
That flows by the throne of God."

The Preacher waved his right hand with the rhythm and led the singing without the need for a book. He'd sung the song a thousand times and the words poured forth with a milk and honey ease. He gazed across the fifty or so souls who ventured out to hear him, out into the heat when they didn't have to. That gave succor to the Preacher. When people did things of their own accord, outside of their own comforts, he knew they were open to the treasures laid up in heaven.

He locked eyes with many of them, one by one, and noticed the glee at singing for Jesus, yet he also saw the tears over the unseen sins of lost souls, those who arrived broken from emotional pains. Those were the ones who looked away quickly, the ones who carried their burdens with them. The Preacher hoped that the power of the Word would flow through him and help heal what he didn't see. He was a messenger sent to save souls and offer succor.

As the voices in harmony grew louder, two boys snuck out the back of the tent and across the parking lot. They ran to the rear of the store where they liked to explore for soda bottles and anything else that might've been discarded. Both boys spied the empty RC at the same time. Jacob was faster but Levi shoved him out of the way, so hard that the younger skidded on the ground and bloodied an elbow against the hard-panned dirt.

Levi and Jacob were the Preacher's sons, and he took the two of them wherever he sojourned to share the gospel. They traveled the roads between Tennessee and Kentucky in a brown 1957 Ford Ranch Wagon bought with money left to the Preacher by a favored uncle. It was just the right size with a back seat for the boys and a covered bed where they carried the tools of the minister's trade: paper goods, bibles, tracts, and songbooks. If necessary, the wagon bed served as sleeping quarters when the motels were full or too far away, or the night too cold for a tent.

The Preacher and his sons traveled the hollows and valleys of hillbilly land with the Word of the Lord, and he kept the boys busy handing out fliers, passing the communion trays, and setting up the tents. Levi was fourteen and Jacob was three years behind him, but their personalities were much further apart. Levi liked cheeseburgers and fun, while Jacob was the quiet reader and duty bound to the father. Levi kept a switchblade comb in his back pocket that he liked to run across his teeth and irritate his brother, while Jacob preferred to collect rocks and bottle caps from the ground.

"Ow!" Jacob yelled, then sat up and looked at his crimson elbow.

"Aw, just lick it," Levi told him.

Jacob fought back the tears that would only invite more derision from his brother. Levi grabbed the bottle, but instead of keeping it for deposit, he threw it and smashed it against the brick wall.

Levi looked proud at his work, then turned to see his little brother and the trickle of blood that ran down his elbow. He pulled Jacob up to his feet, took a handkerchief out of his back pocket, and put it to the bleeding bump.

"You tell Dad, I'm gonna give you something else to cry about."

"You didn't have to do that!"

"Come on," Levi said to him. "We gotta get back before the closing prayer."

Together the boys scrambled across the parking lot and ducked under the rear of the tent just before the singing and voices went quiet.

The Preacher paused and gazed across the flock in front of him.

"Before we part ways, brothers and sisters, I want to encourage you to lift yourselves up with prayer, steady prayer, and to walk the straight and narrow. We know not when the Lord's return will be, though Lord willing, my boys and I will be back with you sometime soon."

The crowd smiled, spoke their amens, and rose when the Preacher lifted his arms skyward.

"Let us bow our heads in closing prayer."

PREACHER, 1962

The hot summer gave way to the cold embrace of winter. The snow fell hard and heavy and dampened the sound of an old Chevy truck that bounced across the ruts and disappeared at the curve out of the town. All the homes were shut up tight and covered in a blanket of white, except for the chimneys that smoked and burned to keep their inhabitants content. The high school was the biggest brick building in town and would be the host to tomorrow night's basketball game with a city rival just across the county line, a welcomed crowd if it wasn't canceled by the weather.

The homes here were small and intimately close, built up by jobs in the local factories, making shoes, truck parts, and lunch meat. Each house had two framed windows, a front porch, a swing, the occasional flag, and a basketball goal that hung from a pole or tree. They either faced the dirt streets that ran toward the high school, or toward the road behind the coal mine a few miles away from town. There was little to no traffic as today was Sunday, and it remained the day of rest in these parts, to where it was hard to find any consumptions of any kind for sale.

There were several churches around for such a small place: a testament to the richest days of the community and a penchant for having one's God of choice. Even if the weather dropped below freezing, the locals would get out and go to church. It was a duty, an obligation to God and to share some faith in the local high school basketball team. Others just got bored and wanted something to pass the time or the chance to gossip with a few friends.

Preacher Johnson was known for traveling the circuit of these small towns and professing the gospel to those who were lost or wished to break the monotonous existence of their souls. Preaching was a good and honest living, and the Preacher often brought his boys with him to keep them occupied and out of trouble.

Now, the Preacher rarely had an actual church building to preach from, so he would rent out a room that could occupy at least thirty souls. It could be a funeral home where no one had died close to the weekend, or an empty classroom in a school, or a shuttered store on the old main street.

This town had a gas station that was closed Sundays but near enough to walk to. The glass front windows barely kept the cold away and a small electric heater glowed bright in the corner. If he could pack enough people into the open bay, their bodies would warm each other up, and if he could stimulate them enough with his words for heaven, he could collect a little extra for the holiday season. Most people were in a giving mood about this time of the year, even more so to counter the sins of the previous eleven months.

That's how the Preacher made his living, moving his boys back and forth, and spreading the good news. Word of mouth carried weight and if the Preacher got to the right person, the tongue was better than the devil's workshop. It was a guarantee to get neighbors from a few blocks around to attend the sermons.

They called him Preacher, Reverend, or Minister. He preferred the simplicity of Preacher, though he answered to all of them with a nod, a smile, and a warm handshake, sometimes a hug. There were certain things he liked about each town they passed through. He liked the grocery store where the meat man came to the meetings and brought him butcher paper-wrapped packages of mixed sausage and hamburger. The next town over had a new post office with its rows of shiny gold letter boxes, polished floors, and a gleaming flagpole. Another had the community bank with the big wooden double doors and a safe that covered the wall, and a main street big enough to host a JC Penney that had two floors of merchandise, a tailor, and about anything that could be ordered from the catalog.

The Preacher felt at home in these places. In the evenings and on the weekends, people were likely to run into each other on the sidewalks carrying groceries from the IGA, or leftovers from the A&W, and they would say hello to the Preacher and treat him and his boys like they belonged. There was always someone willing to get extra credit with God and take them into their homes for a few nights as well. There was the red-headed spinster who kept the house she inherited in immaculate condition for all the emptiness it held. It was two floors with the vaulted ceilings and the radiators that heated each of the eight rooms. If they needed to go to the bathroom, plumbing standards had not yet reached the second floor. If the urge came at night, the Maxwell House coffee can was close by the bed. The place was simple and warm, and the Preacher and his boys stayed there each year they came through. Conditions were different in every town they hit. It might be the loft in a barn in a remote area, or a room in an attic or the motel on the side of the road. Rarely did the Preacher have to pay for any place they stayed.

When he needed a break from his boys, the Preacher would send them down to the local library where they could read the latest *Boy's Life* or *Sporting News*, or *National Geographic*. Occasionally, if they stayed in one place long enough or knew they'd be back in a month or two, they would check out books. Levi was partial to stories about sports and cars and playing the guitar, while Jacob was keen on adventure and mystery and comics. Some towns were big enough to have their own movie theater, sometimes a drive in, and the boys saw *National Velvet, The Ten Commandments, Ben Hur,* and *Shane*.

By the time the weather turned warm, they'd visited groups of believers from the north of Georgia to just south of the Mason-Dixon line, living off the good will of Christian folk and the word of God.

"Hope we'll have a good crowd," the Preacher said to his boys as he gazed out toward the little houses near the main street and putting his hand against the glass. "You all finish getting those chairs set up. Make the rows nice and neat now. Don't just do it without thinking about it."

Levi and Jacob dutifully set up the metal folding chairs aligned six across, depending on how many chairs they could find, whether they were indoors or out, and the size of the space they had to work with. There was always to be a row up the middle for those who wanted to come forward for forgiveness of sins and a laying on of hands and prayers. The number of songbooks they carried had dwindled over time and the boys were to put one on every other chair and keep an eye out for attendees who forgot to leave them behind.

The Preacher looked toward the sky for a premonition about the snowfall and the temperature.

"Lord, if it be your will," the Preacher prayed, "let 'em come, Lord. Let 'em come."

The boys glanced at their father as he made his way outside.

"Too cold to be out today," said Levi. "Maybe nobody will come, and we can leave early."

"Maybe that pretty girl will come," replied Jacob, the younger brother, teasing his brother for a reaction.

"Shut up," Levi told him. "You don't know anything."

"Dad told you not to tell me to shut up."

"Well, shut up then."

"That's enough, boys," said the Preacher, stepping back into the empty gas station. "I can hear you both outside. Don't want anyone hearing such foolishness."

With the chairs put out, they set a table up front with the gold-colored communion plates and the weaved giving basket that appeared as a crown of thorns. The Preacher took his place again out front of the empty station and let the snow fall on him while he waved at the occasional passing car with his bible or at the curious eyes from the windows. He spotted a small portly woman walking her way up the road, short and built like a bull with a heavy overcoat, a shawl pulled tight around her head, and clinching hard on her bible for support. The Preacher smiled as he recognized the approaching figure.

"Come on in, sister," the Preacher called out to her. "The Lord surely looks in favor on those who would brave today's weather."

"Good to see you too, Preacher," she answered with a smile. "Didn't know if you were going to be back this time."

"If the Lord desires it, then I return, sister. It is good to see you."

More of the people came. The tall and the thin with the overgrown stubble and the dirt under the fingernails. Men with a green tint to their face from too much drinking. The blind woman who had a special affinity for the Preacher and would tap her way through the snow and the uneven road to get there. There were those with no particular affiliation but in need of everyday prayer, and a few just looking for a better warmth and some words that made sense.

The boys stood near the door and helped to greet and sit the flock just as the Preacher instructed. They knew their jobs in each town, for they'd done it a hundred times. The Preacher planned to speak today on forgiveness. This was a town of more down-and-out people than the well-to-do. They needed parables and words of encouragement, not too much fire and brimstone. Usually, it was Wednesday when he'd pray on the topics and let the Lord lead him to the right lesson, then he'd spend time contemplating the scriptures, in the station wagon while driving or in a local diner over a breakfast special, and he'd prepare the right things to say. He used bible commentaries and pecked away on an old typewriter that was kept in the trunk. He rarely made mistakes because the typewriter didn't correct mistakes. Sometimes he paid for one of his lessons to be hand-painted on chalkboard-sized sheets. He hung the sheets with tacks and used them as a guide to preach the lesson. The people appeared to like the heavenly sheets because they could follow along easier with the Preacher's message. Most of all, they knew when the Preacher would be closer to the end.

There was a chill in the gas station with a heavy scent of motor oil and lubricants. They kept their coats on, even when the message moved into hell's fire. The Preacher taught how men crave for a free pass but are reluctant to give one in return. How pride, envy, gluttony, and all the deadly sins work to separate man from man, and man from God. He worked hard to tell a story with just the right scripture, and he preached until he felt he'd touched at least one soul present. He judged their head nods, the shouts of "amen", and the sleepy and wandering eyes to see how far the message had traveled.

"And so I ask you, brothers and sisters, if you yourselves need forgiveness, if you have a burden that you've been holding onto, a festering wound that will not heal, then come forward, and let the Lord know. Join me as we stand and sing."

As the Preacher led them in the closing hymn, the boys knew to rise and prepare to pass the communion around. The blonde hair girl made eyes and smiled at Levi, and he tried to keep from looking her way since he stood in front of everyone. The Preacher gazed across the rows of faces and felt a sincere appreciation for these people. Some hung their heads in contemplation, while others nodded along and kept pace with the Preacher's singing. These people had come when they had no necessity to do so. They had come on a cold day to hear the Preacher and he enjoyed both the symbol and pride that came with being a man of God.

With no one coming forward for redemption, the boys passed the trays up and down the rows. Today's menu comprised small pieces of broken unsalted crackers and grape juice; much easier than finding a loaf of unleavened bread. Sometimes an older woman from the town, bent upon holy tradition, would bring a fresh square lump of unleavened bread, and if it was near the holiday season, the occasional bottle of wine would be served as well. With a pinch of the bread and a thimble of wine, the body and the blood of Christ were thrown down the hatch in dutiful contemplation of sacrifice.

When it came time to pass the offering plate, the boys handed the communion trays to the preacher and picked up the small round baskets made of brown, intertwined vines.

"You gotta set the example," the Preacher had counseled them prior, slipping each one of them a quarter. "These people like to hear the word, which is good, but the word doesn't live without bread and water and gasoline. Put these in and let our brothers and sisters see you do it."

Levi slipped a nickel into the basket instead. Jacob placed his quarter in like a dutiful son and they passed the baskets along until the rest of the earthly offerings from the people filled them. When they took the baskets back to the front, the Preacher placed them on a small table and covered them with a white linen cloth.

With the final song sung and the closing prayer given, the Preacher dismissed the flock back to their earthly abodes. He hugged his worn leather bible to his chest with one hand and stood near the door and let his other hand dangle free to shake hands.

"Enjoyed it, Preacher," a small balding man said, with his hat off and a firm shake.

"Good to see you again," the Preacher replied with a genuine smile and a pat on the back. "Everything well on the farm?"

"Oh, been a good year, better than last, I reckon. Got two new calves and a good store for the winter."

"Well, that is a blessing to hear," replied the Preacher. "Stay steadfast in prayer now."

"I sure will," the man said with a slight bow. He donned his hat and left.

"Preacher?" one lady asked, with a raised eyebrow. "I've got venison, beans, and cornbread if you and your boys want to come over for lunch?"

"Much obliged, Ms. Jenkins," the preacher answered, keeping hold of her hand and sharing a long look with her. "Much obliged."

MEN OF THE TIMES

When the March winds roared across the land, they carried the Preacher and his boys into the small towns and hamlets along the Kentucky-Tennessee border. Several of the local brethren snoozed during the lesson and the occasional cough or hack told the Preacher that the common cold was in attendance. He cut the lesson short, and with the collection taken up by the boys, the Preacher raised his hands toward the ceiling.

"Let's close tonight by standing and singing number 345 together."

The small group rose with jerks and movement and brought the songbooks up under their noses.

"*So, I'll cherish the old rugged cross,*" they sang. "*Until my trophies at last I lay down.*"

As the choir of voices continued, the two boys fidgeted in their chairs and giggled at a man with his handkerchief hanging out the back of his pants. Jacob used his songbook to conceal his face so the Preacher wouldn't catch him laughing. Levi pretended to blow his nose and stuff an imaginary hankie in a pocket to entertain his younger brother.

The Preacher held his bible and sang the number by heart. He noticed the boys cutting up. He'd embarrass them if needed, but most of the time, they'd get the message and return to their duties as orderly, faithful sons.

With the service over, the last of the saints departed to walk home or pile into the old Fords and Buicks.

"Give y'all a lift, Preacher?" a thin, bald man with a beaked nose and pinched glasses asked.

"Think we'll walk it, brother. We're staying just down the road."

The men waved to each other, and the Preacher and boys began their evening stroll to the boarding house two blocks over on Randolph Street.

"Daddy, you ever think about finding one place to preach at?" asked Levi.

"Why do you ask?" replied the Preacher.

Levi looked toward the ground before answering.

"These people go home," Levi replied. "We go someplace else."

The Preacher thought about the question and looked ahead.

"I know you boys tire of all the riding around. I hope someday you'll see the benefits of the seeds being planted. And you two have already experienced more of the country than many of these folks will ever have a chance to. Besides, there's not enough on the mountain anymore to make a living."

"I thought a long time about staying there and being a farmer," the Preacher continued, "but my father, your grandfather, said my heart was somewhere else. He said, 'son, you better head down to the valley, or consider joining the military. Figure out where you fit in.' So that's what I did."

"That's when you became a Preacher?" asked Jacob.

"Not directly," he continued. "The war over there was an awful thing. Too many troubles too fast. Things I don't think a man is supposed to see. You could say I made a deal with God."

"What do you mean?" asked Jacob.

"It means I swore to God, if he got me off that island alive, then he could have the rest of my days."

Jacob glimpsed a red and white neon sign lighting up the sidewalk ahead, the only place still open this evening.

"Can we get some ice cream, Dad?" asked Jacob.

"You want ice cream on a cold night like this?" replied the Preacher.

Both boys nodded. "Well, why not? A chocolate-dipped ice cream cone sounds good to me."

The business had a walk-up window with a menu displayed to the side, though the Preacher never scanned the menu and just order three chocolate-dipped cones. A car drove by now and again and the buzz from the neon lights above them kept up a steady hum. The Preacher paid with some coins from the collection and passed out the cones. They continued their walk in silence until a disheveled man worn away by the heaviness of life shuffled toward them, one foot in front of the other, waiting for them to get closer. He smiled and waved.

"Evenin," he said.

"Evening," the Preacher replied.

"Say, you wouldn't have a bit of change to spare, would you?"

The Preacher paused, then reached his hand in and pulled a pocketful of change out. He offered it to the man without counting.

"I appreciate you," the man offered. "I'm almost home now. You all have a good rest of your evening."

"You as well," the Preacher replied, and the man continued on his way. The Preacher noticed Levi still watching, still observing the man until he disappeared into the dark.

"What's on your mind, Levi?" the Preacher asked his unusually quiet oldest son.

The boy looked at his cone as he spoke, desperate to re-engage on his initial question.

"Why do all this work, travel around and everything, just to give the money away?" he asked. "I think he's going to get a beer or something."

"Maybe so," the Preacher replied. "The Lord works in mysterious ways. Who knows whether that might've been an angel in disguise?"

"I don't think so," Levi replied. "I think that man will take the money we worked for and get something to drink. He ain't goin home."

"Maybe so," the Preacher replied.

Levi waited for the Preacher to offer more explanation and was disappointed when none was forthcoming.

"Can't you get a regular job, Daddy? The kind that lets you stay in one place. We could go to a regular school and wouldn't have to worry about money and things."

The Preacher did his usual pause and mulled over a response.

"When your mother was alive, many a place wanted us to stay and settle down. They liked your mother really good."

The Preacher stopped himself. He didn't want to return to the past. He tossed the rest of his cone into the bushes.

"Your Mom and I once drove from Muskogee to Nashville in a Ford Fairlane. The car started overheating, so I had to pull to the side of the road. The snow came down so thick, felt like we were in an Eskimo hut. Never a complaint from your mother. It was the Lord's will, she said. Two days, we lived in that car. Got to know each other pretty well. Soon enough, someone came looking for us. Took us all the way back to the mountain in their own truck."

They reached the boarding house as the boys finished their cones.

"You all finish up your ice cream before we get inside. Don't want to leave any kind of mess to clean up."

The boys did as suggested and crunched down the last bites. Jacob took his father's hand and together the three of them walked up the steps to the boarding house. The Preacher hummed to himself, thinking of the passage of time, the boys, and the possibility of a future spreading the gospel that didn't include the road.

THE PITCH

The smoke from the cooker on the corner of Prairie Lane and 9th billowed a steady stream skyward. When people in the little town saw it, they knew the meat was sizzling and the Sunday services were near completion. The café was within walking distance of nearly every congregation and near capacity by the time the Preacher and the boys made their own three-block jaunt from the church where he'd delivered his lesson.

He never said it, but the Preacher liked to hit this town on the circuit through Tennessee. It reminded him of genuine hope and faith, and of grilled liver and onions, and this church was new and growing. The building was envisioned as a church first and not an after the fact empty gas station. The people had pooled their funds together and built their own building with fifty hand-hewed pews and a baptismal that opened under the floor and topped it off with a nice little steeple like the Preacher had grown up with. Now, all they needed was a minister, and they liked that the Preacher was young with two boys, but they wished he could find himself a wife. A biblical preacher needed a biblical wife to go along with the flags on the streets, the barbershop on the corner, and the liver and onions smothered in brown gravy every Sunday.

"Preacher, that was a mighty fine lesson today," offered the man who served as an elder when he wasn't farming his fields. His wife shook her head in confirmation of the fine lesson and kept quiet while her husband did the talking.

"I tell you, Preacher, this place is growing. It's a good place to save souls. Even got a new school going in. Wouldn't you like to settle down some? See your boys in a brand-new classroom? Possibly find yourself a wife? We've got several widows. Real salt of the earth women."

The Preacher cut a bite of the liver, then dabbed it into the mashed potatoes and gravy before forking it into his mouth. He chewed it down before he spoke and spied his boys outside playing on the sidewalk.

"Your offer is appealing."

He cut into another piece of the liver with a knife and fork.

"But I am cut from the mountain, sir. I am, how do you say it, too country. I can bring a few lessons every few months, but more than that, the people would grow tired of hearing my voice."

"Oh, come now, Preacher. I see the way you work a room and talk with the brothers and sisters, and those boys of yours? Why, they would fit right in. This could be a place to lay down some roots. What do you say, Preacher?"

The man smiled after his words, then looked toward his wife for support, who nodded along with him. The Preacher was the shepherd the flock wanted, perhaps even needed, yet no matter how well he preached or prayed or sung, he knew it would never be enough.

Brother Bailey wanted more zealotry in the preaching. Sister Mathis liked to keep an eye on other members and catch them doing sinful things. Brother Roberts thought the Preacher was long-winded, and then there were the disagreements on baptism, musical instruments, and colored members. The Preacher found it best to do the Lord's work like a trucker. Get in, deliver the goods, and get out.

The boys loitered outside along the sidewalk and perused the parking lot, looking for bottles or a dropped penny or anything else that caught their eye. Levi stood between the parked cars and a brick wall and kicked at an empty milk carton until it stood on its end. He jumped on it and made it pop with a loud sound. Jacob looked around the parking lot until he found his own milk carton in the bushes. He set it up to copy his brother and raised his shoe to smash it. Levi pushed his brother out of the way and crushed the carton with a quick stomp instead.

"Why'd you do that?" yelled Jacob.

Levi smiled at his own actions and searched for something else to grab his attention.

Jacob found another carton. He shook the ants off and set it up. When Levi came over to jump on it, the boys tussled. Levi shoved his brother and Jacob fell and hit his head against a brick wall. He cried and grabbed his head as the blood ran down his hand and alarmed him further. He ran back into the little crowded cafe while Levi watched him go.

GOLGOTHA

The journey through life is a series of endless distractions and forgotten moments, like learning to tie a shoe, a soft rain on a sunny day, the drops of water in a kitchen sink, or the scurry of a squirrel across a yard. That emptiness is given little value, so we fill our lives with things that portend toward meaning, some ultimately worthwhile but mostly mindless, as long as the present swiftly enters the past.

The Preacher was not a planner per se, and he let the offer from the liver and onions town linger too long. He depended upon prayer and the invisible hand of the Lord to guide his decisions. Everything happens for a reason. Nothing was left to chance or question. Surely, he thought and prayed, the Lord would provide the right opportunity near the old homestead. He and the boys could live off the land and settle down with the markers and remains of his kinfolk. The simple log-hewed home built by his father would be there, and the church constructed by the mountain folk with the small steeple and wooden cross might get used on special occasions.

Several years had passed since the Preacher last drove up to his old homestead, and it alarmed his senses at how quickly nature or man had reclaimed the land. He searched for familiarity where dark rings framed the trees and the branches reached naked toward the sky. The underbrush was burned to a level he'd not remembered. When the clearing in the distance came into view, he could see the frame of the old home was scorched to a skeleton with the windows blown out. The steeple atop the church teetered and creaked with the wind. While most of the building survived the burn, the roof was settled like a wave and the cross atop the steeple hung at a sharp angle, pointing parallel across a blue-gray sky full of clouds. Ill fared the land that the Preacher had once roamed.

"What happened?" asked Jacob, while his brother picked up a stick and swatted at the ground.

The Preacher looked toward the cracked earth and a weed sprouting between clumps of hard, crusted dirt. He bent down, removed his hat, and picked up a clump, thinking about the father that cut his living from the woods around them.

"Vengeance is mine," the Preacher muttered, trying to discern the reason for such unforeseen events.

Could it be the Lord was cross with him? Was he selfish for turning down the liver and onions church, or was he supposed to stay on the road to preach the Word? Was he being tested like Job of the old book, and this was the beginning of the trials and tribulations to come?

"We'll have to pray on this, boys," the Preacher finally said. "Pray for forgiveness. Pray for understanding and accepting his ways."

"Did we do something wrong, Daddy?" asked Jake.

Levi elbowed his brother. "Don't be stupid. Somebody set a fire up here."

"I don't think so," the Preacher quipped. "Wildfire. Probably a lightning strike. I remember my father talking about it. Only thing that ever terrified him up here. He'd notice the animals moving, the birds, even the snakes. He knew something big was happening."

The Preacher walked a short distance away to a trail toward the family cemetery, where the tombstones and rocks stood cracked and blackened. This was the land of his parents, and their parents, and a few others of the family lineage that had returned to the dust, the same place he expected to be laid when the time came.

The boys followed close behind, a trail they had taken as babes when it was canopied by thick trees and briars and purple vines and long golden spider webs. They watched as the Preacher stepped quietly and carefully between each plot. He stopped in front of one and wiped away the soot.

"Here's your grandparents right here," he told the boys as he wiped the names clean. "And over here is the sister I never knew, born in stillbirth. Over there's my Uncle Charlie. You never knew him. He was my favorite uncle."

"What happened to him?" asked Jake.

"The gas took something out of him," he replied. "That was the first big war. He used to give me dimes all the time. God bless him, he was never the same after he came back. My mother called it shellshocked. She didn't want to let me go when my time came. When I got back, that was after the second big one, I understood some of what he must've experienced. But he was already gone. I would've liked to have talked to him again."

The Preacher gritted his teeth when he came to one last stone. He kept his back to the boys and wiped away more dirt and ash from the name of the wife who'd gone to glory too early. Levi carried a faint memory of the mother who played piano and loved to sing the mountain songs to him. Jake was too young to feel the weight of the void. The boys looked on as their father laid a hand on the stone and hung his head in silent prayer.

Looking back on this moment, the sons did not recall that their father showed any emotion at the conditions of the land, nor had they any understanding that their father might feel his own sense of homelessness without the mountain. They just knew the one place they'd ever heard of as home was no longer there.

"Not much left for us up here," the Preacher said as he stood and held his hat in both hands.

"What are we gonna do now, Daddy?" asked Jacob, searching for answers like his brother.

"Don't know right off, son," the Preacher replied. "I think we should pray on it a bit."

"Can we get something to eat before we pray?" Levi added.

Jake didn't like his brother's boldness with their father, but he was hungry, too, so his silence offered a unified front.

The Preacher put his hat on and looked toward the darkening sky.

"We better start walking to the wagon now," the Preacher told them. "Won't be any place open by the time we get somewhere."

The Preacher took one last look at the homestead. He gently tossed some dirt from his hand, turned, and didn't look back.

THE VALLEY

For the Preacher and his sons, the summer of 1965 would be the last on the road. They traded in the flat tires and the variability of the people from the small towns for the whims of a few Christians to congregate in one place. The Preacher never told the boys about the offer from the liver and onions town. He heard the church had found their man, complete with the pretty wife and a baby on the way. The Preacher wouldn't regret it. Regret, doubt; those were acts of little faith, the seeds of the Devil. Instead, he prayed he could convince enough brethren to come together and form a church in the valley below the mountain. A place that he could tend to full-time and offer some stability for his growing young men.

The valley ran five score miles west from the mountain, and the Preacher hopscotched his way through the towns looking for the right place to settle down. He dabbled in being a security guard, but he didn't like guns. He gave social work a try through one of President Johnson's poverty programs, but the scale of the problems overwhelmed him. He bagged groceries and enrolled the boys in their first public school. He put feelers out, wrote letters, and made phone calls from the booth out front of the local IGA.

Several churches were looking for ministers, and they tried the Preacher out, yet no matter how Christian the people purported to be, it was personal preferences that mattered the most; no beards, wrong suit, dirty shoes, yellow teeth, divorced, single, too Northern, too aged. The people looked for their own hint from God that this man was or wasn't the chosen one. Most wanted a young married couple ready to multiply, while the Preacher was in his fifties and past his prime. Still others wanted a man with a regular job, who could then preach on the side and on the cheap.

And then there was the problem of the "glass house." If the Preacher was on the road, the boys didn't have to deal with prying eyes or whispers. If they acted up somewhere, the Preacher could nip it before they got to the next town. Staying in one place meant the show was on, and these boys, well, they were feral. They'd never had a proper education. If the boys acted in a manner not up to snuff by local members, whether hormones raged, or a curse word slipped, or they said something considered ignorant, the Christians would hear about it and expect a public demonstration of remorse. The boys would be the sacrificial lambs for righteousness, and Levi was already testing his boundaries.

The Preacher thought on starting his own church, where he could mold expectations and realities a bit more. People were always starting their own churches. They'd break off from one another when a bible verse took on a different meaning, or someone was called by God in a more unique manner. Members simply tired of each other and shopped around for a new gathering or a different shepherd.

The Preacher parked the station wagon for good in a place called Middleburg, a town with no significance beyond being at the crossroads of the past and the future. There were plenty of empty buildings and wounded souls. He chose a vacant shop that fronted an old highway and close to the new interstate. The competition was a Baptist church five blocks away and a Catholic parish. Growth would follow the road, but the Preacher didn't wait. He traveled to the south side of the town to find members, where the railroad tracks segregated the people and a white minister coming to them was both an anomaly and a curiosity.

The building had a capacity for 60 souls, so the boys put fliers on windshields and the Preacher got on the local radio station at the crack of dawn and would give little nibbles of his sermon and invite people to come out on Sunday. He visited the area Kiwanis and Rotary clubs and led their opening prayer. Soon, the Preacher had an average of 35 attendees, depending upon the weather and the ending of Saturday night follies.

As time went by, they settled into a routine and the old carpet building became a home in the back and a church in the front. The boys enrolled in nearby schools and had to test for the proper grade to go in, and the Preacher bought his first new suit and a new hat to go with it. The garb was a crisp navy blue with light golden stripes and a white button-up shirt underneath. He could not remember when the last time he spent money on clothes (he'd wore the suits of old brother Bailey after he'd suffered a heart attack while fishing).

The Preacher wasn't the only new thing in town. A store called Walmart set up shop at the crossroads and drove a stake through main streets of the little towns all along the region. People flocked to the cheaper prices and enslaved themselves to a bargain. There was no need to depend on men like the Preacher, no need to know the area butcher, or the owner at the hardware store, or the ladies in the clothing department. Instead of turning toward the Preacher and the Word for guidance, people asked for help in aisle nine.

The Preacher adjusted his tie in the mirror, then sat down with a newspaper in the back of the building. He paused and gazed through the showroom front windows at the occasional cars that would pass by. He considered this was the first time he had settled down since, well, since he'd been widowed, since his old family had passed, and since the place on top of the mountain had perished. It was a sense of abandonment. Didn't matter how many times he preached. Didn't matter what he did or what he believed. There was no place that felt familiar enough to be a home. The road was the escape from all that, but now the Preacher's life wasn't his anymore. His sons needed their own roots.

Levi was quickly on his own path in the little town and made fast friends of the wrong kind. He was a good-looking kid and before long it exposed him to things the Preacher and the roadshow had kept him out of. Local kids gave him an initiation beating and Levi took up smoking in the boy's room, stealing for his new friends, and lots of little things that his father paid for and tried to fix with prayer. Levi wanted to belong, but it was too late. He was rootless and adrift, with no starting point and no ending. There would never be an actual place called home.

Jacob avoided such unpleasantness and remained dutiful to the weekly worship services to support his father. He resented his brother for his selfishness; the way he skipped services now, smoked in his room, and drank straight from the milk carton. Levi complained of his new life after complaining of the old and showed no sympathy for the efforts of the Preacher or his little brother to make a go of it.

"This place is crummy," Levi said, letting the door slam behind him as he entered the back room.

"Levi, if your mother was alive, she'd wonder what kind of father I'd been with you," the Preacher said.

"Hell, Daddy," Levi answered.

"Don't curse," the father interrupted.

"There's nothing to do around here but get in trouble."

"You're an idiot," Jake chimed in.

"Why don't you shut up," Levi retorted.

"Why don't you shut me up," Jake countered.

"Why don't you both be quiet!" the Preacher roared.

It wasn't the first time the boys had disagreed and squared up. The Preacher rose from his cushioned rocking chair, threw his paper on the ground, and stood between them. He turned to look at Levi.

"You think you're a man now? Doing what you please? Coming and going when you want?"

He turned toward Jacob.

"And you think everything in life requires a response? Are you so easily provoked?"

The Preacher traded looks between the brothers.

"We're trying to make a go of it here. What do you think prospective church members would say when I can't control my own sons? Why would anyone listen to the word of the Lord or an old fool of a man when my own sons don't?"

"I'm sorry, Daddy," Jacob offered, looking away from confronting his brother.

"I'm tired of this," Levi added and moved toward the door

"Where are you going?" the Preacher asked

"Does it matter?"

"Levi!"

"Why'd you pick this place?" Levi turned toward his father to say. "There's nothing here. These people are hopeless. This place is dead. You all just refuse to see it."

"Could be this place chose us," the father countered.

"That's baloney," Levi retorted. "You didn't have to come here. You could've tried something different instead of dragging us here to preach. I would've rather stayed in the car or figure out something to do on the mountain. I'd just as soon live and die up there than to come to a place like this."

Such questions and thoughts were foreign to the Preacher, for he had been a dutiful son himself and never questioned his own father or an unseen God in such a manner.

"And stealing from the flower shop?" the Preacher asked Levi. "Was that something you did? That you felt called to? You going to blame that on me?"

"Wasn't like that at all," Levi said.

"What about stealing a car and driving over tombstones in a graveyard? Is that your idea of making things better? How you treat a place? Dammit son, can't you see the opportunities in front of you?"

Levi's eyes grew wide, for he was unaware that the Preacher knew about the graveyard incident. Both the boys stood frozen, for they'd also never heard the Preacher curse.

"You think I don't know things?" the Preacher continued. "Just an old mumbling man out of touch? Why do you think you're not in trouble right now? I'll tell you. It's by the good graces of the people in this town, and by God, there's good everywhere, if you seek it out."

Levi looked toward the ground for the proper response, and to his brother who looked on with scorn, but some things Levi didn't have an answer for. He shrugged his shoulders. His life had been chosen for him up to this point, and he felt compelled to rebel against it. The challenge to set his own course was strong, perhaps because the Preacher was so compliant, so non-confrontational. So *boring*.

But it was more than that. He had his own emptiness, either born with it or thrust upon him by life's absurdities. A sense of loneliness from the mother who'd died young, or the constant churn of places that had festered the void.

"I didn't ask to be part of this," Levi retorted. "Don't even know if there is a God anymore."

Anger flashed across the Preacher's face before it found a home in Jacob, who moved forward to challenge his brother. The Preacher pushed Jacob back and took a deep breath to regain his composure. Defiance was one thing, but blasphemy? Might as well burn books.

"Son, I think you've about outgrown anything I can do for you," he said to Levi. "It hurts me to say this, but it might be time for you to go out on your own. Find what you are looking for. And if you can't do that, there's a recruiter who comes downtown every other Saturday."

Levi masked the hurt and swallowed. The Preacher had given up and called him out. The military represented the order and rules he felt Levi needed. It was a great paradox. A trade between the peacemakers and the warriors in God's name.

Jacob glanced from his father to his brother. His own anger did battle with sadness. He was in pain from Levi's unending defiance but also the thought of his brother leaving them. They'd been together, the three of them, for so long. It was just a wearing down, the ticking of time, and the crash of old ways and thoughts against the current of change.

Levi heard the words of his father, but he heard his own voice, too. He left in a hurry and let the door slam behind him.

The breakup of the Preacher and his sons did not begin at this moment. The boys had simply outlived being sons, and the Preacher had outlived what he knew of being a father. Fathers and sons, faith and forgiveness. The Preacher spent more of his time at the little church in the old carpet shop, listening and praying and hugging. He gave Levi up to God and the institutions of the American government. He was Isaac in the desert, putting faith in the unknown and in calloused men he had never met.

Jacob carried on being the good son and attended to his father's needs with the singing and the communion. He too began the drift but found faith in more acceptable terms of a steady girl, books, and a plumbing license. It was Levi who squandered his freedoms too easily. The authorities stopped him and a car full of miscreants hot rodding in another town with friends and illegal refreshments. Encouraged to find fresh meat for the conflict, they expedited the young men to the recruiter, who told Levi he was leadership material, and he could wipe the charges away. Could get him in officer training once he got through boot camp.

Levi ruminated about that now. How quickly he moved from being a teenager to a grunt in Vietnam. That's the string that got pulled. From the road to the whip, kill or be killed, in the name of the Lord, and all these things might get added unto you, or at least you died trying.

LEVI, 1968

With the papers signed and the prayers said, young Levi mushed back his hair, crushed out a last cigarette, and stepped on a bus for boot camp. Everything came hard and fast now. The swamps of the South drowned out the patient and soft-spoken words of the Preacher. The army broke Levi Johnson down until he had calluses on his elbows and knees. They taught him three things: how to drink, how to smoke, and how to kill, and they changed any faith he had in the unseen, to seeing the enemy first with a well-oiled rifle and a quick finger.

Vietnam was hot, hotter than hell, and in the steamy highlands of *An Khe* it was a kill or be killed existence. The concept of shooting at someone for a cause was a blasphemy to everything Levi remembered the Preacher urging: vengeance is mine, love thy enemy, turn the other cheek. Out here, God was put on pause. Men still prayed and carried their tokens but there was no God to be seen or heard. Out here one dared not to trust or tempt fate. One just survived, a day at a time. That's all that mattered. Not pride and not country. Staying above ground and breathing was the goal.

"Watcha doin there, Johnson?" came a voice from across the way.

Levi let the cigarette dangle from his mouth and tightened up his rucksack. That was Buck. A man-child from the same South as Levi, but not like Levi. His voice was loud and ignorant, full of a false sense of courage. No one knew his real name, only that some brass had called him Buck for the way he pranced around the field, and it took.

Levi and the rest of the platoon ignored Buck as much as they could. He'd exhausted them with his loud, obnoxious banter and his cant-wait-to-get-out-there mentality. There was always that one guy in the group that loved it, and the other men knew he was a danger. He was a hunter who had a desire for raw meat, and what was good for the men around him was only of secondary concern.

"Haven't had any action for a few days now," Buck continued. "It'll be real soon. I can smell the gooks. You know that aroma, Johnson? Like sweat, piss, and soy sauce."

Buck cackled at his own words. Better not to interact, Levi told himself. He'll shut up soon or leave, but Levi couldn't help himself.

"No use lookin for trouble," Levi replied. "It'll find you soon enough."

"The sooner we get out there and kill the sonsabitches, the quicker we can get home. What do you think you're here for anyway?"

"I ask myself that question all the time," Levi responded. "And until I know the answer, not gonna rush somewhere I don't need to be. Not in any hurry to die."

Buck shook his head. He didn't understand. This was the dream. A real-life Cowboys and Indians. Buck turned his attention to another soldier. Fresh meat from Minnesota. A boy who barely fit his uniform. Eugene was not his name, but the rest of men bestowed it upon him. It fit his quiet mannerisms and the way his brain seemed out of sync with his body. He liked comic books and didn't mind eating field rations. The boy stumbled his way through assignments and routines. He was readily gullible to the ways of the real world, and people like Buck preyed on him.

"What's wrong there, Eugene?" Buck jested with him.

Eugene looked up from a comic book he was reading, then pushed his glasses back on his nose and looked at the dirt.

"There's nothin wrong," Eugene replied.

"Well, are you ready to fight? Ain't gonna do shit with your nose in a girlie magazine."

"Th-this is not a girlie magazine," Eugene said.

"Whatever," Buck replied. "If you're near me in a fight, you sure as hell better be shootin or I'll jam the end of this rifle right up your ass."

"Leave him alone," Levi interjected.

"Shut up, Johnson," Buck said back to him. "Not gonna have any light-weights in my vicinity that get me killed. You see, Eugene, you don't have time to mull things over out there. When shit hits the fan, it is kill or be killed, and you better not get me killed."

Buck racked his weapon, and the kid startled and looked between his legs at the ground and then back to the comic book.

"Tell you what I'll do," Buck told him. "I'll make you a hero. You stick with me. I'll help get you home. You can go back to your model rockets and transistor radios. Maybe even get a girl. You ever been with a girl, Eugene?"

Buck chuckled to himself as he slung his rifle over his shoulder, then glanced at Levi and walked away.

Levi wiped the barrel of his rifle with cloth and oil.

"Hey," Levi called to Eugene. "Don't pay him any attention."

"Oh, it's ok. I'm used to it."

"Where you from?"

"Highland, Illinois. My family grows corn and raises horses."

"Is that right?"

"I raise rabbits, too. My little sister is supposed to be watching them until I get back."

"Rabbits, huh? I've eaten a few. My daddy knows how to cook and clean them. Showed me once, but I don't much care for the stink."

"I told my sister not to name them," Eugene continued. "My father says it causes too much attachment. Makes it harder to sell them."

Levi listened with a cigarette drooped from the corner of his mouth and continued cleaning his rifle. He observed the kid reading the comic book intently and it made him think of Jacob. Probably at home reading a comic book himself.

"Did you sign up or get drafted?" Levi asked.

Eugene looked up from his comic book and pushed back his glasses.

"I enlisted," Eugene answered. "All the men in my family have served. My father says even my sister can join when she's old enough, but she wants to be a veterinarian."

Eugene was unused to conversation, but he forced himself.

"How about you? Did you get drafted?"

Levi wiped the barrel of his rifle one more time and put away the cloth.

"Not exactly," Levi answered. "It was either here or jail."

"Huh," Eugene grunted.

"And sometimes…"

Levi slung his rifle and rose to move.

"Jail sounds better."

The kid looked away, then back to Levi.

"It's Frances," the kid said. "My name is Frances."

Levi nodded and left. He didn't want any more conversation; just enough to show some camaraderie, but not too deep. It was a schizophrenic existence; wanting to be fully alive but not to care too much if it didn't work out that way. The times were quick, fleeting, and dangerous, and not meant to be squandered on feelings. On watch in the jungle at night, hell, they couldn't even smoke, couldn't sleep, didn't hardly eat. It was the nerves. From the frying pan into the fire. Into the belly of the whale.

Levi coped with his thoughts and doubts and expectations through liquor, pills, weed, anything that made the days and nights numb. He'd think about the places he wanted to see or getting a girlfriend. He wished he'd cozied up to one before he left so he'd get a letter or two from someone other than the Preacher. Anything to pass the time away and help turn his brain off.

On this day, his unit traveled a familiar route upland. The same piece of land they'd trekked across too many times already, always to fall back for some unexplained strategy or objective. That was hard on the men. It made little sense to give up one of their own for a yard of dirt, only to give the ground back with another body or two attached.

The place was akin to walking a graveyard for Levi. Over there was where Fregosi bought it. He was from California. That's all Levi knew. All he wanted to know. A stone's throw ahead was where Adams dropped. Adams was from Boise where all the family farmed, and all the family did their turn in the military. The men had called him Tater.

"What do you all grow up there in Idaho?" one grunt asked Adams.

"You tryin to be funny?" Adams responded. "What do you think we grow?"

"Oh, I don't know," the grunt replied. "Peanuts? Rice?"

"You stupid, or somethin?" Adams asked.

Levi liked Adams, but he didn't want to like any fellow too much. They sent Adams back in one piece to the family cemetery to rest near the potato fields. Took army forensics forever to figure out where he'd been hit. They found him lying on his side like he was taking a nap. *Gave up the ghost*, as the Preacher would say.

Then there was George, or sometimes they called him BBQ. George looked older than he was and spent considerable time explaining the complexity and beauty of cooking meat on an open grill.

"Have to keep the meat moist," George relayed to anyone with interest. "Keep yourself a spray bottle and an injector. I've got my own recipe. It's a secret though."

George always kept a Winston, lit or unlit, dangling from the corner of his mouth. When he spoke, it sounded as if he was gargling rocks.

"I'll get him," was the last words Levi heard George gargle, then George dropped his long, gangly body to the ground and crawled through the underbrush. George was always the one who drug out the dead comrade. He was going to mortuary school when he got back, a different kind of meat, he'd joke. When George disappeared, there was no sound, no shots, nothing. That really got to the men. It was one thing to lose a comrade, but to lose all of him was something different.

Today, the only clatter was the small cracks of litter under their feet and the grunting of equipment. The platoon slipped through the forest floor by hand signals. When the sign was given, each man paused and spread out to the closest bit of cover the jungle afforded.

"What's goin on?" a scared Frances whispered to Levi, not clearly seeing the signals ahead.

"Nothin," Levi replied. "Hold your place."

"No, he's telling you to come up ahead," Buck interjected from ten feet away.

"Me? Why?" Frances asked.

"Hell, if I know," Buck answered discreetly. "Get up slowly and move about ten yards over here to the left of me."

"Don't listen to him," Levi told Frances. "He's making shit up."

Frances was nervous and unsure.

"God's honest truth," Buck continued. "I've got one sighted about fifty yards, but he's too concealed. Once you move, he'll move, and when he does that, I'll get him. You'll be just fine."

"It's bullshit," Levi said to Frances. "Stay there."

Levi looked up toward the crown of the dense forest trees swaying in the wind, at the palms and teaks crossing paths and closing the canopy further. He rotated his eyes to the left and to the right. A noise, a feeling; something had him on alert, but he could not see what Buck saw.

"Get over here to my left!" Buck whispered again to France. "Move it before we lose the opportunity!"

"No, stay here!" Levi grunted to him. "He wants it so bad, let him go."

"Look Frances," Buck insisted. "I've got your back. Help me flush him out."

It was the first time Buck had used his real name, and Frances gripped his stock tight with sweaty hands and struggled to his feet. Levi saw the kid rise from where he was. Frances stayed low as he'd been taught and moved for cover as quickly as his legs could carry him. He was about twelve steps forward when the shot ripped through him, and he collapsed straight forward with his weapon still in his hands. His face slammed into the wet, moist earth. His foot jerked and Levi watched the steam rise from the limp body.

Another shot rang out and Levi observed another man from their unit go down to his right. Bullets zinged back and forth, and Levi ducked his head to the ground. He turned toward Buck. The brute cracked off three shots, one after the other, and the enemy soldier pin balled down a giant *po mu* tree and thudded to the ground.

"Yaaaahhhhh!" Buck yelled, rose, and moved forward.

The pop! pop! pop! pop! of automatic fire cut all around them as each emptied their arsenals against the other. Levi joined in, firing here, firing there, crawling, turtling, running, hiding; anything to avoid a too quick trip to eternity.

"Hold your fire! Hold your fire!" came a call from the haze.

Buck moved forward quickly, excitedly, and Levi looked back to the area where Frances had been left on the ground. They'd moved thirty yards in sixty seconds, a blur in time, and Levi observed the nonchalance, the psychopathy of Buck, who reached his kill and turned the enemy soldier with his boot.

"I got you, you rat-eatin bastard," Buck sneered over the dead man.

He bent down and rifled through the pockets of the man, scattering cards, papers, money, and pictures to the ground.

The squad leader signaled to rise, and the men slowly stood from their crouched and hidden places. Others kept in place and glanced around for more enemy.

"Shit, these gooks carry nothing of value," Buck pondered.

Levi rose and returned to Frances and turned him over. There was no bringing the kid back. There was nothing left to do, and he couldn't fathom it or think any further. He gazed ahead at Buck, bent over in his pursuit of prizes. He felt a fury build inside and stepped quickly back to confront the beast.

"Vengeance is mine," Levi said to himself, unexpectedly and unplanned. He drew near and raised his gun toward Buck, almost there, before another soldier intervened and put his hand on the barrel.

"Whoa," he said to Levi, and lowered it.

Buck looked at them, missing the substance of the act.

"You say something, Johnson?"

"You got that boy killed."

Buck kept digging at the body.

"He was dead as soon as he got here," Buck said.

"Stifle it!" the Lieutenant called to them. "VC are probably out there listening right now. You all get your shit together and set up a perimeter. You and you, go back and get Eugene. Find out who else was hit."

"His name was Frances," Levi interjected.

"Whatever the hell it was," the lieutenant replied, and strode away.

Buck used his knife and pried the Vietnamese man's mouth open and wrenched a gold tooth free.

"Wow, I thought these bastards were poor," Buck said out loud, then removed a small bag from his pocket and pulled the string. He dropped the gold tooth in with the rest of his mementos, then put it away.

The other men pretended not to see anything, though they all thought the same. *Crazy. Buck is crazy. War is crazy. Get me the hell out of here.*

They scattered, leaving Levi and Buck and the soldier between them. The soldier tugged at Levi and pulled him away. *Like a bottle cap*, Levi thought to himself, his steps heavy like bricks. Two men passed them carrying Frances.

What is the purpose?

The voices competed for Levi's attention. The void between heaven and earth, the knowing and the unknowing. The army hadn't prepared him for this. The voices had warned him. It all seemed so pointless.

What is your purpose?

Why?

But why not?

END OF INNOCENCE

The flares, the shadows, the scratches of lightning in the sky all played hopscotch on the minds of the men, hunkered down in dugouts wrapped high with sandbags and ribboned with mud. The Viet Cong made life miserable with nightly rocket attacks and perimeter infiltrations.

But Levi Johnson had stayed alive. After two years, he was a boy with the memory and experiences of an old man. He had twenty-eight days left in country. Faces had come and gone with the swing of the body bags, the clipping of dog tags, yet he had his golden ticket, and the men avoided him like he was fresh meat. As a short timer, no one wanted to get in the way of the cosmic pendulum. Their young minds kept singularly focused on avoiding any temptation of fate and upsetting their own getting out and getting gone before they were culled. One lesson was baked in. No amount of prayer offered protection from death.

Even the lieutenant thought it a bad idea to go out. A colonel from further back flew in with his companion dog and his handlers and demanded an increase in patrols.

"We are seeing a lot of nightly activity," the colonel chewed the words as he spit them out, his little dog sniffing the ground in and between the men. "I need you all to ensure the enemy knows we're here, and that we will take the fight to them."

The men listened at attention, ignoring the bugs flying about and their senses frayed to questioning the strategy of any order from on high. Vietnam made no sense. Grunting about, endless up and down, and getting killed on someone else's credentials. Their job was to give up the present for a better-future tomorrow, for someone else.

"The 2nd battalion has given hell to the enemy just north of here," he continued. "There's lots of chatter going on, lots of movement. I suspect the enemy will probe for weaknesses on the flank, which takes them straight to you. Hold your ground, men. That's an order. Lord willing, we can wrap this up and be home by Christmas."

And how ironic that men would be cold in the ground somewhere back in the states before the colonel's speech was finished. Levi heard the voices in his head.

Upon this rock.

The words of the Preacher he'd heard a thousand times from a thousand lessons. Holy ground where men built temples to talk with their gods. Where men spilled blood in the name of currency and land.

Hold your ground.

Levi listened to the voices. He could taste the moisture of the earth. He spit dirt from his mouth and his eyes adjusted to the bursts of light and explosions. His ears rang from the chatter of gunfire. He could make out a few of the men nearby, and there was Buck. His eyes caught Levi's, and he smiled a sinister smile and spit tobacco.

Buck dropped to a knee and hugged up close to a bent palm. He scanned the canopy for his favorite prey, the man in the trees who stayed concealed, and picked the unit apart, one by one, as they passed. Buck sunk all the way to the ground. He was an excellent shot, a predator, and the men in the trees were in season. He used the litter to balance his rifle and scan the treetops. He moved his rifle slowly, scoping in anything out of the ordinary, until he caught a small piece of glistening flesh. It was an ankle, or a hand. Possibly a patch of uncovered neck.

Buck dialed in his target. He anticipated the victory and the new trinkets for his collection. So engulfed by his own shadow, so believing in his own superiority, he didn't see the actual shadow of the enemy coming up from behind.

But Levi did.

The army had trained the men to react with stealth and do it quickly, and Levi twisted his weight and his weapon toward the crawling threat. Levi would remember admiring the man as small, sinewy, and capable. He had green khaki shorts and a loose-fitting shirt caked with dirt. The man slithered along the ground with the movement of a serpent and clenched a knife in his mouth like a long tooth.

The ticking of the clocked slowed. The movement of the man halted, and despite the potential benefit of the carcass being Buck, Levi controlled his emotion and shifted. There was time.

The shadow came forth from the dark. The knife came up slowly. The man coiled to strike.

Levi cracked off one shot. The man was close enough to Buck that he collapsed dead on the back of the brute's legs.

Buck yelped and turned in an instant and beat the dead man with the butt of his rifle. He breathed the rarified air of fear and vulnerability that he normally shook off with hubris. That was too close. That was... embarrassing. Worse than getting killed, Buck had wet his pants. He looked down at his soiled britches and around for other living evidence of the shame, then he saw Levi.

Hell damnation. They exchanged glances, and Buck understood Levi had both saved him and exposed him. He couldn't live with it. His mask had fallen. He lay his rifle aside, unsheathed his knife, and stood despite the danger. His eyes locked on Levi, his mouth closed, and his face melted to menace.

Levi could've shot him. *Should* have shot him, but the power of the Preacher's words and the red line between murder and killing moved his hand toward his own knife. Levi lay his rifle down, stood, and unsheathed his blade.

Buck smiled with a sinister greed. *My ground. My trophy.*

He charged and thrust his knife toward Levi. Levi caught him by the wrist, and they rolled entangled across the lush, dark, sacred ground. They swiped and lashed and kicked and the shadows dissolved around them, and the blood ran. The war was a whisper, and it was just the two of them and the angel of death.

They gripped onto each other for their lives. Levi could smell the stench of the beast. He felt the strength of the larger body. He feared failing, and an animal instinct to survive made him bite down on Buck's ear. Buck roared and stabbed at Levi, catching some tissue and bone in the back of the neck.

Levi ripped the fatty meat from the lobe of the predator with his teeth. Buck's guard dropped at the violence to his own flesh, and for just a moment,

Levi gained an upper hand, turned his own knife, and plunged it in. He laid his weight on the weapon and pushed until Buck bellowed and shook from the intrusion, and his hand came down like a claw across Levi's face. Levi sweated and gasped for air and pushed until the blood ran dark and Buck's fingers dug into the ridges of Levi's skull.

Their hearts beat faster and faster while the seconds dragged until Buck's strength faded, and he whimpered at the betrayal. Their eyes locked and Buck's last moment filled with shock, for no man really knows the hour that the Lord cometh.

Buck's mouth set open, his eyes drifted to the right, and the bit of life left in him floated away. Levi rolled him off in a heap and swiped at the blood pouring from his own wounds. He heaved with deep breaths, crawled away, and turned over. He caught sight of stars in the sky and a moon that cast light into the shadows of the treetops.

There were no shouts for help. No further movement around him. Sporadic gunfire had crept ahead, and a breeze rustled through the understory around him. Levi heard his father's voice. *The unseen hand of God.*

With cool sweat running beads down his face, Levi could hear his heartbeat in his ears, and he swallowed while the jungle seemed to come alive with the buzz of cicadas. He was unsure of how much time passed. A minute? Five minutes? An hour?

He looked at Buck's lifeless body and the work of his own hands. He felt an evil pride, a sense of justice. It was a different feeling of freedom, or a new cage, he didn't know which.

He wiped his blade off on Buck's vest, then patted the brute down until he found the hidden bag inside his jacket. He pulled it loose, pulled the string open, and tossed the trophies like scattered ashes across the ground, then he picked up his rifle and rose and left Buck's body to the ashes and dust of the earth.

KING OF KING, 1975

Levi awoke while it was still dark and blinked at the rusted springs of the bunk above him. His sleep was never sound, never deep, and only good for that fleeting moment of time when he would awake without the disappointment of knowing where he was.

God-damn this place.

Levi got his bearings and looked across the cell to the bunk where the scrawny kid slept. Not only was the kid awake, he was staring directly back at Levi.

"What are you looking at?" Levi asked him.

"You was talkin in your sleep, but I really couldn't make anything of it. Except Jesus. I heard you say Jesus. Don't mind me. I was only wonderin with your daddy being a preacher and all and, well, I was thinkin on it and wanted to ask, what are you doin in here anyway?"

Levi laid an arm across his forehead and thought about the question before he replied. "This ain't the place to be curious."

The sound of the door drew their attention. They observed Burns pass by the bars and walk down the hall. The early morning ritual. Coffee, breakfast, check on the inmates, go have a smoke. They waited until they heard the door open and shut again.

"How old are you?" Levi asked.

"Eighteen."

"Don't you go worrying about why I'm in here. Real question is why you're in here?"

"Drinking and driving, but I wasn't drunk. That John Wayne wannabe pulled me over and pulled me out of my truck. I was about to fall, so I put my hand out to steady myself and ended up grabbing on to him. He said I swung at 'em. He punched me right in my face and then added an assault to my charges. Can you believe that? Bunch of bullshit is what it was. Sheriff said he'd cut me a deal."

Levi knew the real meaning and what the kid was getting himself into. He looked back across to the kid.

"Listen real good," Levi said. "There's no deals here. No matter what they say. You shut up and do your time. Don't get involved in anything."

"I see you coming and going," said the kid. "I'm not spying or anything. Just passing the time. I was hoping I'd —"

"What?" Levi asked.

"It's like this. I've got a girl. Thought I might get some time to see her."

"You wanna see your girl again? Be a ghost in here. Don't get seen. Don't be heard. Don't think."

The second hand on the hanging clock turned slowly. It didn't tic-tic-tic like most clocks, but moved in a smooth, flowing arc around the face. The kid nodded and shrugged his shoulders.

"Man, I am hungry."

Levi reached into a crevice between the wall and the bunk and pulled out a pack of powdered donuts, then tossed them to the kid. The kid tore open the pack and gobbled them. He wiped the powder from his face and licked his fingers.

The clank of the door reverberated down the hall. Footsteps clapped on the concrete floor and grew louder. Burns arrived at Levi's cell and stopped.

"You got a visitor," said Burns.

Levi hesitated, then climbed down from his bunk. Most likely the Preacher, he thought. Running late, off his usual schedule.

"Well, where is he?"

Burns looked away and motioned with a head jerk. When the steps ended, the brothers eyed each other.

Years of frustration reflected across their faces. They'd not seen or spoken in many months.

"Listen up," Burns said to both of them. "This isn't visiting hours and I don't want any attention drawn to it, so keep things quiet and civil, got it?"

Burns stared the brothers down, then clapped away in his shiny shoes down the long cold hall.

"What brings you here?" Levi added.

"Need your help," Jake replied.

This was odd. Levi leaned against the bars. Jake glanced towards the kid, who rolled over and went back to the donuts. The brothers looked at each other, sizing up the differences chiseled by time. Levi noticed a bit more weight on his brother, more of a presence. This person was still his little brother, but certainly more of a man.

For Jake, Levi was a lost cause. He was gaunt and pickled from self-abuse. Tattoos marked the stops along the way. He had been trouble since the moment the three of them had settled down, and the army had done little more than discharge him home with more ways to cause trouble.

"Did you bring any smokes?" asked Levi.

The selfishness of the question caught Jacob by surprise.

"Are you shitting me?" said Jake. "Haven't seen you in God knows how long and that's all you got to say? Not how are you doing? How's the kids? How's Dad?!"

"Leave the drama for somewhere else," Levi replied. "Why are you here?"

"I'm here about Dad."

"What about him?"

"He's dying," Jake said. Levi didn't move, simply taking the words in with his breath.

"What do you mean, dying?" Levi asked. "He was here just a few days ago, doing the usual."

"Heart attack. Old age. I don't know. He's at the regional hospital. Not getting any better."

"Nobody told me. Why didn't you tell me?"

"Since when do you get phone calls? Besides, it's not my job to keep you up to date. You wanna know things, then stay out of jail."

"You think you know everything, little brother."

"I know I don't have the luxury to not give a shit. Whatever this excuse for living you've become, at least you don't have a family to drag along with it. I'm glad you weren't that stupid."

Levi tried to hide that the words hurt. He hung his head and felt his pocket out of habit for a cigarette. The boys had been so used to their father being around, full of spirit, being the peacemaker between them, it was a hard thing to settle with.

Jake had long ago stopped making excuses for his brother, living with the reality that Levi would suck up most of the relationship that existed between the three. But his father's presence had also allowed him to keep a distance; to keep the craziness at arm's length.

Levi ran a hand along the length of his arm and scratched his head.

"What can I do?" Levi said, and he put his hands on the bars.

"You gotta get yourself out of here," Jake replied. "Help me take him up the mountain."

"Not that easy."

"Figure it out. I know you've got something going on with the sheriff."

Levi looked up at his brother, startled at his insight.

"Don't act so surprised," Jake continued. "I hear things. You've been in here for what? A year? Eighteen months?"

Levi darted his eyes and hushed his tone.

"Sheriff made shit up. I was only selling some weed. Not even that much."

"Sounds typical," Jake replied. "You're an innocent bystander."

"Didn't say that," Levi offered. "Just trying to do the time and get out of here."

Levi looked to the floor and mulled over his options, mostly how he would handle this with the sheriff.

"How bad is he?" Levi asked.

"Can't be long," Jake answered. "A couple days."

"Shit," Jacob muttered. "We can't let Daddy die in the hospital."

"There is no *we*. It's only me, unless you figure a way out of here."

"Dammit, Jake, this is no time to get all high and mighty with me."

"I've done my part, brother," Jake replied. "I came here to tell you. I'll be at the hospital. One way or the other, with or without you, I'm doing this."

Jake took a few steps down the hall and Levi hit his fists against the bars in frustration.

"Bring some damn smokes next time!"

Jake stopped and turned back toward his brother.

"You see, that's what I mean," Jake replied. "You're a selfish sonofabitch. One of us has to do something, and I guess it's me. You wanna see Dad again while he's alive, you're gonna have to do some time for someone other than yourself. In a couple of nights, I'm taking him out of there and up the mountain, with you or without you."

Jake walked away without looking back. Levi watched him go. His brother was right about everything. He knew it, but he wouldn't admit it. It pissed him off.

Levi called after him, "I'll kick your ass when I get out of here."

"Yeah, you look like you're gonna kick a whole lot of ass," Jake replied over his shoulder.

Jake rounded the corner and out of view. When the big door clanked open and shut again with a bang, quiet held the hallway.

"Shit," Levi exclaimed, and he looked back toward the kid, who turned away quickly, then put his head against the bars.

CHOICE OF THE PRODIGAL

Burns and the other guard worked on 12-hour shifts. That's the way the sheriff wanted it, and he hired mostly former military men for all his positions. Men used to authority and order without too many questions. The one he kept around the longest was Burns. Burns was never late, never complained, and took overtime and extra shifts like he could exist on two hours' sleep a day.

The sheriff changed the shifts regularly, some days early, some days late, with some weekends. It kept everyone on their toes. The exception was Burns who took the shift no one wanted; the dead man's shift from 6pm to 6am. It suited him and the sheriff. There were fewer people for Burns to deal with and less paperwork, and it allowed the sheriff to keep a couple more officers on patrol for contraband.

Sheriff Price relied on Burns, more than he'd admit, but he never gave Burns a higher rank. People might think Burns was next in line, and the sheriff liked expectations kept low. Rank didn't matter to Burns anyway. Someone had to be in charge, and it wasn't in his nature to covet the role of being sheriff. He was a trained company man. It was only when the leader fell that the next man took over. Until that time, you do your job, keep your mouth shut, and keep your eyes on the mission. Burns was that simple. His only crutches were cigarettes and coffee, habits fueled from twenty-plus years in the army.

Burns arrived for his evening shift just as the jailbirds finished up their bologna sandwiches, apple sauce, cardboard cookies, and Kool-Aid. *The Andy Griffith Show* played on the corner television, one of the few shows on the few channels the inmates could watch.

On special occasions, such as the approach of Christmas, the sheriff played charitable and let one of the local civic clubs set up a projector and show old movies. Most times it would be *Holiday Affair*, *White Christmas*, or *The Bells of St. Mary's*. They'd get Laurel & Hardy, Abbot and Costello, and the Three Stooges, too.

It was during *The Bishop's Wife* that Levi heard the clang of the door and the familiar steps of Burn's and the jingle of his keys. Levi tucked the rest of his sandwich in his mouth with one big bite and rose to the bars.

"Burns," Levi said quietly.

"What is it, Levi?"

"Listen, I need to talk to the sheriff about something."

"You know the sheriff doesn't operate like that. You don't ask for him. He asks for you."

"This is different, Burns. Now, hear me out. When my brother was here yesterday, he told me the Preacher was sick. Said he was dying. I've got to get out, Burns."

Levi paused before his next words.

"This is what I figure. I'll make a normal run for the sheriff, and just peel off to visit with my Daddy. Quick and easy."

Burns looked pained and darted his eyes around the cells, then leaned in to speak lower than the television.

"Now, you know not to talk to me about any of that shit you got going on with the sheriff," Burns replied.

"Burns, this is about my Dad."

"You know what the sheriff would say. Should've thought about that before you got in here."

Burns turned to leave, and Levi reached through the bars and grabbed his arm.

"What the hell?" Burns said.

Levi removed his hand.

"He's dying, Burns," Levi said. "Now, I know you don't think much of me. I don't blame you, but I've caused you no trouble in here. My father's dying and I need to see him. Just give me a chance with the sheriff. One chance. Let me make my case with him."

Burns already had a sense from Jake's visit that something was going on. He respected the Preacher. He understood the request, but Burns thought there was no use for Levi to ask the sheriff for any favors. The man didn't grant leniency to the incarcerated, and Burns had no interest in getting crossed up in anything. Yet Burns was intrigued, and he had a streak of honor. For the Preacher's sake, and to balance out whatever the sheriff was up to, he'd give Levi a chance to talk his way out. Burns extended the key, turned the lock, and slid the heavy bars back.

"Move."

Levi exited the cell and nodded to Burns. Burns looked over to the kid, busy watching the old movie and paying them no attention, then slid the bars back in place with a clank.

Burns walked Levi to the end of the hall and stopped at the door as he extended the next key from his assortment.

"The sheriff is here now," Burns told Levi in a hushed tone. "He'll be gone in under thirty minutes. This is how you play it. You'll mop early tonight. You get the mop. You run the water. Real hot. Get some suds going. You get that mop and bucket, and you mop, and when you get near the sheriff's door, you stop, you knock, you listen."

Levi nodded he understood, then Burns stepped in closer.

"This is for the Preacher. That is all. You get in any trouble, you damn well don't bring it back here to me."

Levi nodded again.

Burns stuck the key in and opened the door. Levi passed through, and Burns shut the door and locked it from behind. He observed Levi for a few seconds through the plated glass window, then thought better on it and moved back down the long corridor.

Levi went straight to the janitor's closet, a place he'd been many times as the lone trustee. He ran the water until it was hot, shook in detergent from a rusted can, and dunked the mop until the water was frothy.

He wrung the mop and plopped it on the floor, then swished the head from left to right in wide waves until he reached the sheriff's door, then parked the mop and bucket.

He took a breath and blew out before he knocked.

"Yeah," hollered the sheriff from inside.

Levi turned the knob and opened the door. The sheriff looked up, not expecting any visitors.

"Did you want me to mop your floor?" Levi asked.

The sheriff cringed with annoyance.

"Where is Burns?"

"He told me to go on and start the mopping."

Levi thought better than to play the charade too much further.

"Sheriff, while I'm here, wanted to ask a favor."

The sheriff put his focus back on the papers in front of him.

"You know the rules."

"It's my Dad. He's in the hospital."

"Not my concern. If I let everyone out who had someone sick, I'd be the one in jail. Now, get out of here."

The sheriff passed a paper to a pile and took another from a different stack.

Levi observed the situation as untenable. He'd done plenty on the whims of the sheriff and still had to guess when he was getting out.

The sheriff realized Levi hadn't moved. He slowly looked up and over his glasses.

Levi squeezed the words out. "I've never asked for any favors, and I've never said nothing to no one about anything. My Daddy's dying and I need to go."

The sheriff felt his blood rise. It was rare to be questioned. It was an unspoken rule. His inmates knew better. The big man studied Levi for a few seconds more, his pulse rising.

"What would you say, Levi? What could you possibly say that anyone would have an interest in?"

Levi swallowed hard at the line that he'd crossed. There was no turning back.

"I've got nothing to say to nobody," he replied. "Just asking for a courtesy to see my Dad."

The sheriff thought for a brief second that he could shoot Levi. *Here's your courtesy*. He could make it appear what he needed it to be. The look on the loser's face would be worth the irritation. His meaty paw balled up at the anticipation; an opportunity to practice his quick draw.

But then he'd create more work for himself. And the mess. Being close to Christmas, he'd be doing paperwork throughout the holiday, and it would cloud the spirit of the season.

For Levi, he had thought about escape many times. All he'd have to do is make a delivery and peel off. He was familiar enough with the details of the jail that maybe they'd let him go and forget about him, that they'd be glad he was gone. He knew enough on the officers and their secrets: when things got picked up and where they got dropped off, and who had disappeared from their cell without warning.

He couldn't fool himself. There was no scenario where he could put enough space between him and the sheriff that the sheriff wouldn't bring him back dead. And there was absolutely no hope in pushing past the sheriff now.

The ask was the only way forward, and he stepped even further into purgatory.

"I've done some stupid things, Sheriff," Levi stuttered. "I've done stupid time for them. One way or the other, I've gotta see my father."

It was the demise of his father and a tinge of guilt that gave Levi the boldness.

The sheriff balled his hands and rose from his desk. Levi tensed for a blow as the sheriff came closer.

The sheriff moved with precision, one step, then another, and lifted one hand like a claw. He gripped Levi by the neck and forced him against the wall.

Burns heard the commotion from the cells and leaned against the door. He put his key in, then stopped. He removed the key and turned an ear to listen further.

Levi choked and he could feel the heat on his skin. The big man's breath bore down on him. The sheriff squeezed until Levi's eyes bulged, his nostrils flared, and his veins popped. It would take only a few seconds to squeeze the life out of this worthless scum. The sensation to kill Levi was strong. It wouldn't be the first time he'd wrung the life from a man. He'd lost count during Korea.

Then the sheriff stopped. He loosened his grip and let go. Levi fell back against the wall and gasped for air. The sheriff sucked his own breath in and wiped his sweaty hand on his shirt. It would be too much trouble. *Goddammit.* Killing this piss-ant like this. Wouldn't be worth the paper, the story he'd have to concoct. He was smarter than this. Power was force and force was control. There was always a better way. Kill two birds with one stone.

"Okay," the sheriff answered his own thoughts out loud, as he took a step back and observed Levi cough and gag for air.

The big man calmly turned back to his desk and sat down. He pulled a handkerchief from his pocket and wiped his hands, then reached a key to the drawer below the desk and unlocked it. He put his beefy hand in and pulled out a paper bag in the perfect shape of a brown brick, then slid it across the desk with Levi's truck keys.

"Picked it up fresh this morning. You know where to take it. Get it done, then get back here."

Levi put his hands on his knees and gasped for more air. The sheriff viewed him with no concern, as if the last minute had never occurred. Levi sat up and looked at the package. It would be back to the Curry brothers, whether he wanted to or not. Levi moved over to the desk to pick up the brick.

"Say hello to the Preacher," the sheriff uttered, with a heavy breath and a sinister smile.

Levi didn't acknowledge the words. He picked up his keys, the brick, and left out the side door. When the door closed behind him, the sheriff got on his radio. He watched Levi get in his truck and start it up.

"Unit 13, you on patrol?" he asked, with a click of the receiver.

"Copy," came the answer.

"Clear the roads. No stops."

"Roger that," came the reply.

The sheriff clicked off and wiped his hands again. This was an opportunity. It would take care of some problems. It wouldn't interfere with his holiday schedule. He'd make sure of it. He had a new kid to mold, too. He switched to the desk phone, picked up the receiver, and dialed.

For Burns, he hadn't heard everything, but he'd heard enough. Whatever was planned would leave no loose ends, and he knew to stay dumb and stay the hell out of it.

THE TRAP

Levi rubbed sweat from his eyes and tried to keep the truck between the lines. He cracked the window to let the cold air hit his face. His hands shook, and he craved the elixir of a cigarette, then fumbled with the radio, before he yelled out with a release of pent-up anger.

"SHIT!"

He drove to the same convenience store he always stopped at and parked away from the entrance, then scrounged for change, hidden cigarettes, and a few bills. He entered the store and bought a pack of Marlboro reds, a cheap Bic, two tallboys, and a Jack Daniels mini, then he took the change, strolled back to the truck, and wasted only two minutes to light a cigarette, chug a beer, and calm his nerves.

Levi crushed the can and tossed it into the bushes, then proceeded to the phone booth at the corner of the store. He put his dime in and punched in the number for the Curry brothers. Wasn't the kind of place he wanted to arrive unexpected. He gave it several rings before he gave up and returned to the truck.

With the second beer gone and the second cigarette lit, he took out of the parking lot with a screech of tires trying to catch on the slick road. His plan was to drop the Curry boys the weed as quick as he could, price be damned, then haul ass to the Preacher. Whatever came after, he'd figure out. He still felt the grip of the sheriff's fat fingers around his neck and tried to rub it away, but it was imprinted, as if the sheriff had marked Levi as damaged goods.

It was a three-cigarette drive to the Curry farm and only the occasional car or truck passed him on the way. Levi wiped his forehead with his sleeve and assessed his odds of surviving the next forty-eight hours. If he could make a clean sell, get the Preacher, and make it to the mountain, he could live off the land, just like the Preacher used to talk about in the olden days.

Then again, the weather was hazardous and no telling the condition on the mountain. There would be no readily available food. Water from a nearby spring might be frozen. Jake would possibly help, then he quickly quelled the notion. He didn't want to be beholden to his little brother and asking could even put his brother's family in danger.

Wasn't worth it. He'd have to come up with a better plan or just run until he couldn't. That was the plan most of the time. He'd been on the move his whole life.

When Levi pulled off the highway onto the windy dirt road, he could see no lights in the old Curry farmhouse. The truck bounced along the rutted road between overgrown fields covered in snow until Levi spied a small flicker of amber orange glowing near the front yard. When the headlights turned at the end of the drive, there was Robert Curry, exhaling smoke and flicking the ash away with his middle finger.

The sight of him gave Levi a sense of dread. Robert took one more puff on his cigarette and flicked it to the ground. Levi gripped the steering wheel with both hands. He could feel the situation weigh on him for a response.

He stopped the truck and kept the engine running, put the gear into reverse, just in case, then he waited. Robert strolled to the truck and Levi rolled the window down in slow fashion until the two were within spitting distance.

"Sheriff wanted a quick sell," Levi offered. "Holidays and all. Bottom dollar. Two hundred bucks."

Robert looked over at the stash on the seat.

"Sheriff was in a giving mood, huh?" asked Robert.

Robert nonchalantly pulled the crush pack from his pocket and pulled a fresh cigarette.

"Want one?"

"I'm good," answered Levi. "Just a quick sale."

"You in a rush to get back?"

"No, no," Levi replied and cleared his throat. "It's just that... my dad's in the hospital. Was gonna go see him... while I had the opportunity."

"Ahh," Robert replied, and blew smoke through his nostrils. "I heard about your old man. Is he up at Regional?"

"Yeah."

"Hmm. I've visited a few people there over the years. My mother passed away there from angina. She smoked too much."

Robert knocked his ash out on the ground.

"My father was there several times. They put him on one of those things with the hoses and the big green tank he could roll around with. He was always moaning about something, swinging his cane at us when he got tangled. He was kind of a bastard. To tell you the truth, when he fell off the porch, I felt relieved, Levi. Almost like it was a Christmas present or something."

Levi nodded and hoped for a quick end to the conversation, then noticed another figure in the dark of the headlights. The other Curry brother hobbled down from the porch and approached them. Richard Curry was the brother everyone knew as the safe one. The one you would call slow, but you never talked about it, not with Robert around. Robert might treat his brother like a dog, but that was his domain, his right.

"You go back in the house, Richard," Robert told him. "Make us up some of those pork chops."

The brother momentarily paused, struck between following an order like he was used to, and stirring against some other force. Robert turned back to Levi to finish his thoughts. He cupped his cigarette for another puff, then he removed a pistol tucked in behind his back.

"There's been a change of plans, Levi," Robert Curry told him.

Levi looked at the gun, then back to Robert, then over toward the brother, who shook his head from side to side.

"Robert, don't you do that," he said to his brother. "Don't you do that to him."

Levi went through several scenarios for survival in a matter of seconds.

"Don't pay any attention to him," Robert quipped. "He likes to get on the phone and listen in sometimes. I don't speak to the sheriff too much. Really got no use for him. Anyway, he offered me a deal, Levi. Said we can have until March to move our product across county lines, unimpeded, whenever we need to. Only one condition. This is the part you'll be interested in."

Levi's body hummed with anticipation. Robert took one more long drag and flicked the butt away.

"He said I had to take you out of the picture, Levi. Told me just like that. Said you'd been overcharging me and keeping the difference."

The blood ran out of Levi's face. It was true, though not that much. Levi knew it was a bullshit excuse; a concoction to get rid of him and everything he knew.

"This is all business, Levi. Supply and demand. Mutual beneficiaries. You know how it is."

"You get out of here, Levi," said the other Curry brother in fits and starts and pointing at his older brother. Richard danced from one foot to the other and put his hands out as if to grab something that wasn't there.

"Robert… is up to no good! No good!"

When he got close enough to Robert, the bigger man stepped aside and backhanded his brother with his free hand. Richard fell to the ground and rolled away. Levi saw his moment and gunned the truck in reverse.

Robert turned back to Levi and shot.

"Ah!" Levi yelled out, as the shot tore into his shoulder. More shots sprayed all around, cracking the windshield, the dash, until the back of the truck banged across a ditch and into a field of frozen, dead corn stalks.

Levi lifted his head. He could see Robert approach him in the headlights with the cylinder open and fishing bullets from his pocket. Levi thought quickly. Forward was the only way out of the ditch. Forward with a turn toward Robert. He threw the column into drive and hit the gas. The wheels spun to catch the ground. Robert peered through the headlights. The truck finally caught in the cold dirty sludge and lurched forward with a screech, then catapulted from the ditch.

Robert slammed the cylinder back in and raised the gun. The truck roared, and Robert took aim for another shot.

Levi ducked. The shot sent another crack through the windshield. The grill of the truck hit Robert square in the torso. Robert grabbed onto the hood ornament. Levi continued forward until Robert's hand slipped loose and Levi mowed him under the wheels. With a bump and a crush, Robert Curry came chewed up out the back. Levi hit the brakes, and the truck skidded to a halt. In the headlights was Richard, on his hands and knees, breathing heavy, scared. *A lost puppy.*

Levi smashed the gas, turned the wheel, and whipped the truck in a circle. He looked at Robert, with his gut punched out and a leg and an arm turned the wrong way. Levi glanced down at his own blood seeping from below his clavicle and put a hand to it. The blood soaked quickly through the shirt, but the bullet appeared to have exited his back. *God, it hurts.*

Levi put the truck in park, pushed the door open, and ambled out in front of the truck. He gazed at Richard, holding himself near the ground, then bent down to pick up Robert's gun.

"Mm-mm…" came a groan from Robert. With his glasses gone and blood splattered across his mouth, his big belly heaved for air. He blinked his eyes to see the blurry vision of Levi above him.

"Where's… my brother?" he sputtered to Levi.

"He's over there," answered Levi. "He's fine."

Robert coughed, and the blood percolated from his mouth.

"Kill him… too," he muttered.

What? Levi thought to himself.

He'd seen how Robert treated Richard. He was his brother's keeper, but more like an abused pet.

"Not today," Levi told him. "Just you," and he sent Robert Curry to hell with one shot.

Levi passed Richard, rocking himself along the ground, and got back in the truck. He put the gear into drive and mashed the gas.

"Aw, Jesus," Levi said to himself, and he put a hand to the hole in his shoulder. He peered into the rear-view mirror in disbelief, as if he could see time in reverse. It happened so fast. Now, what the hell could he do?

He lay the gun on the seat and drove for several miles with the throbbing, aching wound. He rolled the window down and tossed the bag of grass out. He needed help, needed a doctor. Out of the question. No time. He drove quickly to the only place possible, across the county line and out of the sheriff's jurisdiction.

His mobile home was set back from the highway in the corner of an apple orchard. There was nothing there to covet or steal or bother with; nothing of any worth to lock the door for. The rent was cheap, for the farmer saw a renter as an extra set of eyes on the place.

Levi pulled in, shut the truck off, and stumbled out. It was the first time he'd been to his place in months. He staggered up the rusted metal steps, pulled open the outer screen door, and turned the handle. The door creaked when it opened. The place was musty, and he tried to turn the light on, forgetting the electricity had been cut off for some time. No use paying the bill if he wasn't there enough.

He went to the kitchen and dug around for a flashlight, then moved to the bathroom and rummaged through the medicine cabinet before he found a selection of pills. He took what was left in one small bottle, poured them into his mouth, and crunched them down with the help of handfuls of water from the sink. He peeled his bloody shirt off with a grimace, then made his way in the dark to the bathroom, where he located a brown plastic jug of hydrogen peroxide, unscrewed the cap, and poured it over his shoulder.

"Aaaahhhh!" he grimaced in pain and clenched his teeth at the searing burn.

He got on his hands and knees, turned the bathtub faucet on, and slumbered over under the water. It was ice cold, and he shivered from both the cold and being shot, but his wound burned, and the sweat poured from his face. He threw up.

Wash away the sins.

He felt around for a towel and the flashlight, then took a small knife from the drawer and dug for the Bic lighter in his pocket. He heated the blade with the lighter, then poured the peroxide across the blade and watched it sizzle, then set it on the sink and wedged the flashlight into a place to hold the beam. His body pulsated against his intentions and his hands shook. He gritted his teeth, picked up the knife, and laid the fiery blade across the hole.

"Aaaahhhh!!!" he screamed again and held the blade in place until his face flushed, and the tears squeezed out the corners of his clinched eyes. The blood cooked and he felt his flesh burn and gripped onto the vanity. When he sensed he'd done enough, he dropped the knife and slid down to the floor.

He breathed heavily. He'd known pain, physical pain, but not like this, not since the war. He cried out loud at the pain and the tears ran. His mind raced with craziness and his Tower of Babel filled his head with voices until he passed out.

RISEN

It was dark when the knock came at the door. A young black woman. He remembered her from high school. Rose was her name. About 17. She dropped out with just a few months left. Would've graduated. She'd gotten pregnant. She needed food.

"Levi, Jacob, you all sit here with Rose while I go get some things," the Preacher told them.

Levi sat on the couch. Jake tinkered with a radio. Rose sat on a chair by the door and played with her keys. They looked in every direction except each other. Fifteen minutes of nothing. Too embarrassed to breach the quiet.

When the Preacher came back, he handed Rose a bag of groceries. She thanked the Preacher. She left quickly. The Preacher watched her go, then shut the door quietly.

"You didn't ask her anything," Levi said to the Preacher.

"What is there to ask?" replied the Preacher.

When Levi awoke, the blood caked around the wound and his body stuck sweaty to the linoleum. His thoughts momentarily ran to the wounds suffered in Vietnam, and the same feeling of survival in a world turned upside down.

"You've got a nice tattoo now," the medic told Levi, sewing shut the gouge in the back of his neck. "A bit deeper, you'd be paralyzed. Consider yourself lucky and go get you some poontang."

Levi tore himself from the floor, the wound caked up, and swayed toward the back bedroom. He pulled a sheet from the bed and ripped it with his hand and teeth, then wrapped a piece of it under his arm and around his neck. He stopped to probe around the bullet entry and exit, then slowly tied off the ends of the sheet.

The pain, his predicament. It felt familiar. He knew he'd be a fugitive now, once they knew he wasn't dead. The sheriff would say he escaped. It would be easy. Every probable outcome, every conceivable thought, could only end in Levi's demise.

Levi shuffled back to the kitchen. Hell, he'd left nothing to drink, not even a warm can of beer. And what time was it? He scrounged in a nearby drawer for an old watch. The face read five minutes before midnight. He exited the front door quickly and stopped and gazed into the darkness for any noise or movement before he got back in the truck, yet there was nothing but the wind carrying snow through the branches and the distant cracking of limbs.

He had limited choices. The pain continued to radiate. The pain fueled an anger. It wasn't fear. It was an acceptance. A resolve. They had set him up. Sent him to the slaughterhouse.

He turned the truck over. The bottle of whiskey was there. He downed it half-empty. A momentary solace. He could gain some distance if he left now. Go in another direction, get across the state line, but then what? The facts wouldn't matter. The sheriff could spin a tale and every lawman around would want the opportunity to hunt a man down for the holidays. This Christmas could be remembered like no other.

Levi resolved to do the unexpected. If he was going to die, he'd make it painful for the sheriff. Levi wasn't expected back, so there'd be no one waiting for him. It was the only choice that made sense to him. He needed a *get out of jail card*, something to bargain with, and he knew where to get it.

He reversed quickly and hit the highway. The snow fell steady and the wipers acted as a cadence to his thoughts. He gave himself little time to change his mind and drove with abandon given the severity of the weather. By the time he pulled into the jail parking lot, he sweated profusely despite the cold that hung in the air. There was no other movement and no sign of activity. Burns would still be on duty. With a quick breath, Levi stepped from the truck, quietly shut the door, and made his way back to the sheriff's side entrance.

He took his key, unlocked the door slowly, and cracked it open. The odor of the big man still lingered, but the office was dark and empty. He moved in and let the door back gently. He moved to the other side of the desk and sat in the chair. The safe was noticeable even in the dark, the metallic cylinder and the white of the serial numbers catching a bit of light from the glass exterior door.

His plan depended on this moment. He'd watched it many times. He was a keen observer, and the sheriff was lazy about it, careless with misplaced pride. Levi caught a number here, and a number there, and tucked away the probable combination, just in case.

He spun the knob. 32 to the right. 37 back to the left. One time around to 34.

He grabbed the lever and pulled down, but the door didn't budge.

Damn.

Footsteps came from the hallway and Levi pulled the gun from his waist and scurried to the side of the door. He slowly brought the gun up as the keys hit, the knob turned, and the door opened.

Burns stepped in and stopped. Everything seemed in order, but maybe it was the scent of another brand of cigarette, or the cold sweat of fear, or the aroma of blood.

"What the hell?" Burns muttered.

Levi cocked the gun and Burns froze. Somehow, Burns knew, and he slowly raised his hands to his shoulders.

"That you, Levi?"

"How did you know?" Levi asked, gripping the pistol with a sweating hand.

"Lucky guess," replied Burns, though Burns knew Levi wouldn't have been expected back. Obviously, something had gone wrong.

"Did you have anything to do with tonight?"

Burns thought on how to answer. The truth was he had suspicions of a setup, though he had nothing to do with it.

"Levi, I warned you, and you know I don't get involved with the sheriff's arrangements."

It was enough for Levi.

"Get on your knees," he told Burns.

Burns moved slowly.

"May I put my coffee cup down?"

"Go ahead," Levi told him, and Levi quietly shut the door behind them.

"Take it easy, Levi," Burns said, as he placed his favorite coffee cup on the corner of the desk and then used the desk to lower himself to his knees.

"I don't want you getting jumpy and blowing my goddamned head off."

"The sheriff set me up, Burns. Told Robert Curry to kill me."

Burns slowly put his hands on the back of his head, interlocked his fingers, and took the news in. He tried to seem surprised where there was none, but he knew what the sheriff was capable of.

"If that's the case, Levi, why would you come back here?"

"I'm a liability now, Burns. As good as dead, and you know it. But I've got a plan, Burns. I've got a way out of this."

Burns tried to turn a bit to look at Levi and see if he was just plum crazy. Burns' pride hurt for getting jumped but he admired that Levi had somehow survived what the sheriff planned for him. That was an unusual success. Burns eyed the bandaged shoulder and knew Levi was injured.

"Whatever you do, it better be a damn good plan," said Burns. "He will hunt you down. He'll kill you dead, for sure."

"Maybe so, but I'm going to take that ledger, Burns. That's my way out of this. If he comes for me, I'm going to ensure he hurts."

"Don't say anymore," Burns implored. "The man can smell the bullshit. You'll make me a conspirator and I'll be dead before you are."

Burns felt an unusual sense of admiration for Levi. Levi wasn't as dumb as he thought. The ledger was the book of secrets. The off-the-record activities. Burns turned his attention to the first challenge of surviving the next few minutes.

"You're going to have to sell it, Levi," Burns told him.

"What do you mean?"

"Sell it. Make it believable. May I?"

Burns slowly reached his hand out and picked up his favorite coffee cup, then let it fall from his hand. The cup shattered into bits and pieces across the floor.

"I'd rather be alive when this is all over. You'll probably be dead, but he'll still try to blame me. That's how he'll work it. So put a round in my arm or leg. Here or here.

Burns slowly pointed to two spots.

"Not much lower or you'll hit something important and bleed me out."

The request stunned Levi. He was impressed at Burn's matter-of-fact procedure.

"I've got no beef with you, Burns. You've always been fair with me."

Burns nodded. He understood, but he was still angry with himself. Anytime an inmate got the better of a guard, it meant paperwork and whispers about not being up to the job. Burns was a proud man. Truth is, he didn't like the sheriff. The sheriff was corrupt. He did things *unseemly*, and Burns considered himself a genuine type of lawman. He would not die because of the sheriff.

"Get on with it," Burns invited him. "Won't be the first time I've been shot, but it goddamned better be the last. I'm getting too old for this shit."

Levi raised his gun and Burns looked straight ahead, closed his eyes, and prepared for the slug. Levi understood what he was about to do to a decent man, and he couldn't do it. Instead, Levi shifted the gun in his hand so the butt stuck out and bashed Burns hard across the head.

Burns' head tilted with the blow, then he toppled face forward, knocked out cold.

"Not going to shoot you, Burns," Levi said.

Levi moved quietly to the interior door and cracked it open. There was no movement or sound, and he slipped quickly to the janitor's closet and rummaged for tape, then removed a big gray roll and returned to the office. He tied Burns' hands together with several circles, then moved to his legs and did the same. He tore off another piece of tape with his teeth and slapped it over Burns' mouth, then drug Burns to the janitor's closet with one arm and tied him in between the pipes. Levi grabbed the mop, shut the closet door, and wedged it in to jam it closed.

He returned to the sheriff's office and shut the interior door. He'd missed a number. He was sure of the first one. It was the second one that was the problem. *The middle number, dammit.* It would be an educated guess. Sheriff Price had big meaty fingers and the middle number was the one that rolled by quickly.

He spun it until it clicked at the 32, then turned it one time back and stopped at the 38, then forward once more to the 34.

When he turned the handle, the safe clicked open without a hitch.

The sonofabitch.

There was the ledger. The surprise was how much money was there and the time the sheriff had spent stacking and sorting bills and putting rubber bands around them. Levi searched the drawers for a bag and grabbed the one in the garbage can. He swiped the bills into the bag, then paused briefly as he fingered the paper-sized brown ledger and opened the cover.

There were dates and amounts of money. There were names, including two other men he hadn't seen in the jail for a long stretch, then there were his initials, with a line crossed through them. The sheriff had an operation dating back years, and if Levi could put distance in between him and the sheriff, this wasn't just freedom, this was salvation.

The throbbing in his shoulder told him to hurry. He put the ledger in the can with the money, then removed the bag with all the contents. He shut the safe back, pulled the handle up, and spun the dial. He took his goods toward the sheriff's private door and glanced out the window into the parking lot. With no signs of movement, he opened the door and hurried out across the parking lot. The snow was steady, and Levi made a fresh set of tracks back to his truck.

He started up the truck, kept the lights off, and slowly pulled away to the open road. His plan took shape as fast as he drove. He stressed to make it to the Preacher and get rid of his pain, letting his attention drift, but also wanted to gain a few strategic hours on his potential pursuers.

The Piggly Wiggly was close by and would be mostly empty at this hour, except for the few cars and trucks parked at angles up close to the store and the rest along the back row where the employees were told to park. The neon sign of a smiling pig came into view, and he pulled in and drove past the advertisements in the windows for the selection of meats on sale, including a few turkeys still in stock for Christmas.

Levi had been here many times before, to shop, smoke a joint, drop a dime bag, or some other individual endeavor. He crept the truck along until the wheels lined up at the end of the back row, and then cut the ignition.

The vehicles ranged in age from a '57 Chevy to a '75 AMC, with a majority being trucks. He left the keys in his own ignition, got out with his loot, and skirted between the bushes and the vehicles. He checked one by one until he found a door unlocked and got in. This one was a red '72 Ford with a hardtop over the bed, a long neck steering column, and a dream catcher hanging from the rear-view mirror. He put his bounty on the passenger seat and stuck a screwdriver into the plastic hooding of the steering column. He'd not done this act before, but he'd seen it accomplished relatively easily by one of his wrong road acquaintances.

The column cracked and released a tangle of wires. He yanked the familiar ones free and twisted and touched them together until they sparked. It took less than two minutes, and he crept the truck forward with the lights off, turned out of the parking lot, and disappeared.

SAVING THE SHEPHERD

The Regional Hospital was quiet for the holidays, overlaid with lights, wreaths, and ornaments that cast a faint green and red glow across the polished floors. The emergency room had two visitors who sat away from each other, laid back in hard plastic chairs and blowing smoke signals toward the ceiling.

The glitter and brightness made the hospital entrance appear more like a department store than a hospital. Visiting hours had officially ended at nine, over four hours ago, though it was not unusual for loved ones to remain and loiter about as everyone knew everyone and extra time was given to those who wanted to converse with the soon to be dead, most especially near the holidays.

Food was cheap in the cafeteria on the first floor and Jake hung out at an empty square table over a cold cup of coffee and watched the minutes tick toward two in the morning.

The bastard's not coming, Jake mused to himself.

It shouldn't have surprised him, but it did. A part of him had always kept a door of redemption open for his brother; a willingness to abide by the old code of a brother's keeper. As the last straggler left the cafeteria, a janitor came through with a cart full of cleaning gear. Jake took a deep breath and stood up. He tossed the cup in a wastebasket and punched the elevator to the third floor.

The bell dinged, and the doors slid open. The hallways were dark for night hours and Jake walked past the nurse's station without being noticed.

He entered his father's room and closed the door quietly behind him. The Preacher lay motionless, asleep, and appeared thinner and a lighter shade of pale than just a day before. Jake moved to the side of the bed and put his hand on his father.

"Dad?"

The old man stirred with the familiar sound and his eyes fluttered open.

"Are you ready to do this?" Jake asked.

"What?" the old man asked.

"We're going home. Gonna take you up to the mountain."

The Preacher's eyes widened at the mention of the mountain.

"Really?" he asked.

"Yeah, but we have to hurry," Jake replied as he tucked in sheets and rolled medical equipment out of the way.

The old man appeared confused before he nodded and smiled at a thought of the past and closed his eyes again.

Jake removed the lines that snaked up and along his father. The machines buzzed and whirred their disapproval before he pulled the cords from their sockets. He bent over and slid his hands under his father and carefully raised him from the bed. Gently, he placed the Preacher in a wheelchair, tucked the sheets around him as a brace, then wheeled him toward the doorway.

He moved to the door and cracked it open, then gazed down both directions. With the hallway clear, he wheeled his dad out and toward the elevator. So far, so good. As they passed the nurse's station, he avoided eye contact and the nurse from previous encounters popped her head up over the counter.

"Excuse me," she politely stated. "Excuse me. Mr. Johnson?"

Jake sped up, and the nurse rounded the station to catch up with them.

"Sir?" she inquired.

He got to the open elevator and rolled his father in, smashed the button several times, and waited for the door to close. The nurse moved quickly toward them, holding her stethoscope tight around her neck, and the Preacher slowly raised a hand and waved goodbye to her.

As the door slid shut, the nurse turned and moved back to her station. She needed to call security, she needed to check her other patients. She picked up the phone from the desk and dialed the number for security. Waiting for an answer, she looked at the clock, and then put a finger on the plunger to stop the call. She put the handset back in the cradle and tapped her fingers on the table, then she looked at the clock on the wall again.

Outside, Levi pulled in and cruised through the hospital parking lot. He looked back and forth as the wipers squeaked across the windshield. In between the gaps in the rows, he spied the Preacher's old station wagon. He'd made it in time, at least he thought so. He pulled in beside the vehicle as Jake exited with the Preacher.

Levi put the truck in park and got out to greet them.

"Typical," Jake said to his brother, on account of his late arrival.

"I'm here aren't I?" replied Levi.

"Pop the back."

"Got delayed some," Levi added, then shuffled over and opened the back of the station wagon.

"Careful," Jake told him, and together they picked their father up out of the chair and slid him into the back of his station wagon feet first.

The old man exhaled, and Levi looked down over his father and placed his hand on his father's cheek and gently rotated his head in the crease of a pillow. He felt the skin of the old man and the roughness of the whiskers hidden along the pale, smooth places. The Preacher was still there, but the body was giving up. Levi observed how extra old his father appeared, and extra tired, and he forgot his own pain over the age worn into his father's face. Creases of time that ran decades. A pang of guilt crawled up Levi's neck.

"Dad?"

The old man half-opened his eyes.

"Levi?"

"Yeah, it's me, Daddy,"

"Good to see you. What, what time is it?"

"I don't know. Late. But don't worry about it. We're going home now."

"The mountain?"

"Yeah, we're going up the mountain."

Levi grimaced and Jake observed the wrapped-up shoulder and the reaction of his brother. Wasn't the first time he suspected more had occurred than he knew, and he noticed the unknown truck. There was no time for questions.

"Come on," Jake said, "we've got to get a move on."

Levi placed a hand on the sheets and pulled the blanket up. The old man moved his head to look at Levi again.

"I knew you'd come," Preacher said.

Levi nodded, and the brothers exchanged glances with each other.

"Wait," came a voice.

The nurse crossed the entryway and a median, almost slipping and falling on the snow-covered grass, to reach them.

"Please."

Levi shut the tailgate door carefully. Jake turned to her, ready for another effort to stop them. Instead, she reached into a pocket on her white vest and produced three vials of morphine and three syringes.

"When he's ready," she said. "Give him this."

She nodded from fear at her own action. Jake knew what the lady was doing, the danger she was putting herself in. Levi looked on and Jake nodded back to her he understood.

"You better hurry," she said. "I have to make my rounds and do a report."

She glanced across the parking lot and fingered her stethoscope nervously, then moved briskly back to the hospital.

"Gotta stop at the house," Jake turned and told his brother, still annoyed with Levi despite his condition.

"I'll meet you there," Levi replied.

"Don't be late," Jake retorted.

Jake stepped into the old brown wagon, started it up, and drove away.

The clock was ticking now. He viewed his brother behind him in the side-mirror, then turned to see through the sliding glass for his father laying in the wagon bed. With no movement and no alarms, he pulled onto the road. Levi had shown up. On his own time, as usual, but he was there. It still exhausted Jake. That's how it was with Levi. Too much water under the bridge. Too many disappointments. Jake had prepared to move his father on his own. Levi surprised him, and now it was almost an inconvenience to deal with him, too.

JOURNEY BEGINS

Home was thirty miles on a narrow, windy highway, followed by three right turns past a lake, down a rutted dirt road turned to slush, then cut into a driveway through an opening of the sycamores. The headlights found a simple one story with a screen porch, an old place Jake had bought and fixed up to start a family. Jake kept the wagon running for the heat and got out. First out the door was Benjamin, ten years old, and eager to see his grandfather.

"Why aren't you in bed?" Jake asked him.

"Did you get him?" Benjamin asked.

"He's in the back," Jake replied. "You shouldn't be up this late."

Benjamin went to the rear of the wagon and opened the long door.

"Grandpa?"

The old man stirred at the small voice and rolled his eyes up toward the boy looking down at him.

"Howdy," the Preacher said in a soft voice.

"Benji?" came a voice from the porch.

Rachel bounced a baby on her hip. Her long black hair flowed freely across her white robe, and she used a hand to shield the baby's face from the flakes of snow. Jake's wife was the voice of reason in the family, and she was not fully convinced of the plan Jake had cooked up. She didn't like Levi either, which made things worse.

"It's freezing cold out here, Benji," she yelled. "Get yourself back in the house."

Jake walked around to the back of the wagon and joined his son.

"You heard your momma. Say goodbye to your grandpa and let him have a rest."

"Grandpa, you ok here?"

"Pretty good," the old man answered. "How about you?"

Benji nodded and Jake shooed him away.

"I'll be right back, Dad. You doin alright?"

"Yeah," the old man said.

Jake shut the door softly and Benji came back and followed him toward the house.

"I wanna go," Benji implored. "Please, Dad."

"No," Rachel called from the porch. "Come get in the house, Benji."

"Dad?"

"You heard your momma," Jake said, and steered his son toward the house with a nudge. "Don't go and get me into any more trouble. Anyways, it is way, way past your bedtime."

Benji ran inside, unhappy with the answer.

"How long do you think you'll be gone?" Rachel asked.

Jake rubbed the baby's head and admired the curls in her hair.

"Start now and we'll be there by morning," Jake replied. "If he makes it. I just wanna get him there. Let him see the place again. If I can do that, it'll be worth it."

"Did your brother come?"

"He did."

Rachel wanted to be supportive. The Preacher had married them and had always helped when they needed it, whether looking after Benji, paying a bill, and so on, yet the combination of Levi, the weather, and the wish of a dying man made her fret.

"I hear everything you're saying, but I don't like it," she added. "The weather's bad. You haven't been up there in a long time. Who knows what you'll find?"

"Haven't been anywhere for a long time," he replied. "And it's the last chance for him. I gotta do it. I owe it to him."

Rachel gave a heavy sigh and gazed out as the snow continued to collect on the steps up the porch.

"It's your brother that really scares me. Did you ask him how he got out?"

"Didn't see any purpose in doing so," Jake replied.

"Hmph," she grunted.

Rachel handed Jake the baby, wrapped her robe tighter, and stepped off the porch barefooted to see her father-in-law. Jake watched her walk across the frozen ground. How beautiful she was. How lucky he was.

She opened the back of the wagon and stuck her head through.

"Preacher?" she said, and the old man opened his eyes again and looked at her. He smiled.

"Hello… angel."

"Are you in any pain?" she asked, and her emotions caught on her last word.

"No," he answered. "Just tired."

"I love you, Preacher," she said. "You're a good man."

The Preacher smiled.

"Love you… too," he replied.

She kissed his forehead, then exited the truck and wiped her eyes with the back of her hand. She returned to the porch and took the baby back from Jake.

"I want to go," Benjamin yelled from somewhere in the house.

"No," Rachel quickly answered, as the baby startled.

"But why?" Benji replied. "It's Grandpa. And it's almost Christmas."

"Don't argue with me."

Benji appeared from his room with his coat on. He stared down his father, then a sad look crossed his face, and he bolted away from them out the door and across the yard.

"Benji!" Jacob called after him, but the boy ignored his father and disappeared into the woods.

"I can take him," Jake said to his wife.

"No," she answered, bouncing the baby. "He's too young for all this."

"Probably went up in the tree house," Jake said. "He'll get cold and come in."

They turned toward the sound coming down the road. When Levi pulled into view, Rachel immediately noticed the unknown truck, and suspected trouble.

"I don't even know where to begin," Rachel said.

"And I know nothing about it," Jake said to her.

"You didn't ask him?"

"Got my mind on other things right now."

"Well, he's not leaving it here."

Levi drove the truck behind his brother's shed and cut the engine.

"What's he doing?" Rachel asked.

Jake had no answer. Before there were more questions, he ventured into the bedroom for a heavier jacket. Levi hobbled from behind the shed and zipped up his pants.

"You could've come in and done that!" Rachel yelled out to him.

"Kind of late," Levi replied. "Didn't want to disturb anyone."

Yeah, right. Doesn't want an ass chewing. Rachel shook her head at him, and Levi glanced toward the baby girl.

"She's getting big. Where's Benji?"

"He ran off into the woods," Rachel answered, annoyed. "Come on over here, Levi. I want to talk to you."

"No, ma'am. I'm afraid you'll hurt me."

"You come back without my husband, you're darn right I will."

Levi waved her off and tapped his hand on the side of the truck.

"Tell Jacob to meet me over by the lake," he said, then got back in the truck, started it up, and pulled away while he could.

Jake returned to her side with a small bag and a heavier jacket and watched Levi leave.

"He's crazy," she said, as the lights of the truck disappeared into the darkness. "I don't like this one bit. Nothing good ever comes from dealing with your brother."

"Maybe this time will be different," Jake replied. "On account of Dad and all."

Rachel felt a moment of shame. This wasn't about Levi; it was about the Preacher. It was about her husband's father and his wish to take him home. She leaned into Jake and kissed him.

"He said to meet him by the lake. You better go before I give this craziness any more thought."

Jake nodded and kissed her again, then the baby, before he stepped off the porch and into the snow.

"Benji?" he yelled into the woods, but the boy didn't answer.

"He'll come back as soon as you go," Rachel said.

Jake nodded in agreement, then rounded to the back of the wagon, wiped the layer of snow away, and looked in. The Preacher appeared to be asleep. Jake let him be, took one last look at his wife and daughter, got back behind the wheel of the wagon, and pulled out.

WINTER'S MOON

The moon set low in the night sky and was the only source of light across the waters of the lake. Levi pulled up and parked in an alcove of trees and turned the headlights off. The snow fell like petals from a field of blooming pear trees, and he kept the window cracked open for the crisp, cold air and to exhale his smoke. He kept the motor and heater running and spied a lone beaver making a zigzag from one side of the lake to the other.

Levi pulled out the flat, thin bottle of whiskey. He took a long swig and drained it, blew away the bite of the elixir, and screwed the lid back on with two fingers, and laid it aside. He wiped the moisture from his mouth with the back of his hand. His shoulder throbbed a continuous rhythm, and he hoped the whiskey would dull the chorus better than the pills.

Another ripple moved across the lake as the beaver switched directions, and Levi fingered a lit cigarette from the tray and watched it burn between his fingers and thought on the journey ahead. He inhaled smoke, then exhaled. He felt hazy and tired. The last few hours were an intensity he'd not felt for some time; certainly not since returning from Vietnam, but something was different. It was a resolve, a confidence that he'd been missing. He was alive, he had the ledger, and he had the sheriff's money. He had the upper hand. He had a *reason*. If this was the end, it had an ending worth finishing.

Levi rubbed at the achiness in his eyes. He wore his choices and now he was tired. Tired of talking, tired of disappointment, and tired of this life. The thoughts gave him some resolve to get this right. To get the Preacher home.

It was the whiskey and the drugs and the pain talking to him. All the old familiar friends. When Jake pulled up beside him, Levi flicked his cigarette out and cringed from a stab of pain that shot through his shoulder.

"What happened?" Jake asked him.

"What makes you ask, little brother?"

Jake observed the state of his brother and glanced closer at the apparent wound and the make of the unknown vehicle.

"Because you look like shit, and this truck isn't yours."

"Can we bypass the third degree and get on the road? I'm here, aren't I?"

Levi turned the truck off and left the keys, then took a last look at the dreamcatcher. He left the empty bottle, took his cigarettes, got out, and shut the door. Robert Curry's gun was lodged between his back and his belt, and he patted it once discreetly to make sure it was really there. He stopped to look through the back windows at the Preacher, then opened the passenger side of the old brown wagon and got in.

He tried to shut the door softly, but the ancient beast had its own way. The big door needed oiling and didn't catch until he jerked hard to close it. He turned stiffly until his shoulder stopped him, taking in the sheets, the jug of water, the blanket, and a couple of boxes of odds and ends. He could turn no further.

"Packed for the trip," Levi stated. "Just like old times."

"Not sure what we needed," Jake replied quietly. "Didn't know if you were coming either."

Jake caught an aroma of alcohol and observed the sweat on his brother's face. A patch of blood made its mark along the wrapped shoulder.

"Are you shot?" Jake asked.

"Yes."

"Jee-sus Christ."

"I'll explain later," Levi replied. "Get a move on, and make sure the heat is on back there. It's damn cold up here."

Jake observed his brother. Levi was a screw-up, but he never thought him stupid. Whatever had occurred, this was something different.

"Is there anything I need to know?"

"Yeah, but not for the reasons you're probably thinking. We're all here, so can we… get things going?"

Jake shook his head at his brother, gave up, and backed the wagon away from the lake. He turned the wipers on and steered back to the dirt road and toward the highway. He pulled a small round acrylic knob to put the beams on bright. The *whir, whir, whir* of the wipers and the motor of the heater filled the emptiness between them. Not another word was brokered until the snow-covered dirt road ended and gave way to the blanketed highway.

"Do I need to take a back way?" Jake asked.

"Questions, questions," Levi replied, his eyes closed, then added, "we have time. Just go. Highway is fine."

The back tires caught in the mush as Jake pulled out onto the two-lane highway and followed the smooth imprint of tires from previous travelers. He fiddled with the heater until the air felt warmer across the middle vent. The dim lights of the radio pulsed with the heater, and the wisps of smoke from Levi's cigarette left a small cloud above their heads.

"Crack your window," Jake told his brother.

Levi slumped against the window, took the cigarette from his hand, and cracked his own window. He took one long last toke of it, flicked it out, and rolled the window to less than a finger of being closed. The brothers rode along with the hum of the wagon and the motor from the heater. Small talk was foreign between the two of them. The words left unsaid were too much to converse now; too heavy with the brevity of time to crash out into the open. The weight of it all made it difficult to think of what a normal conversation could be between the two.

"So, here we are," said Levi, with his head back and his eyes closed.

There was no reply from Jake, whose head bobbed along with the road as he kept one hand at the bottom of the steering wheel. He glanced in the rearview mirror for any movement or headlights before craning his neck to see if there was any movement from the Preacher.

"We'll stop in about an hour and check on him," Jake said, as he turned his attention back to the road. "I tried to make it as comfortable as I could. He had all kinds of stuff back there. Not sure when they were last moved or used. Hey, are you listening?"

Levi grunted an answer.

"I don't think this odometer is right either," Jake added. "Says he's got 156,000 miles on it. Should be a lot more. Hey."

He called his brother's name but there was no answer, so he tapped him on the shoulder.

Levi grunted louder and moved away from the tap.

Jake turned quickly to assess his brother and a few glances at the wrapping along his shoulder.

"You gonna tell me what happened?"

"Curry."

"Curry? You mean… Robert Curry? That sack of shit? How in the hell did you get involved with him?"

Jake took quick glances back and forth between his brother and the road.

"I told you," Levi replied. "Sheriff was never gonna let me out without gaining somethin. He wanted a delivery done."

"Delivering what?"

"Grass. Weed. Typical stuff. That's what he does there. How he makes money. The jail is just a front. Watch it!"

A big rig blared its horn. Jake corrected as the bright lamps drove by and he skidded back into his lane.

"Well, finish the story," Jake stated.

"The sheriff has his system. They stop people, take their stuff, mostly dealers from other counties. Their middlemen, trucker drivers, and so on. They rat on each other to protect their territory and deliveries. The sheriff takes their shit and sells it. Someone else does the dealing and delivery. That's where he has me. Until I'm released or dead. Then he'll get the next sucker."

Levi padded his pocket in a search of another cigarette. He let his head rest back against the window and sway with the movement while he brought the freshly found stick to his mouth and lit it.

Levi had been a pain in the ass for so long, Jake had almost forgotten how to feel sorry for him. But this was something more. This felt like family again.

"Who shot you?"

"Robert Curry," Levi replied. "By the sheriff's permission. But don't have to worry about him anymore, and that's enough for now. I don't feel like any lectures."

Levi drifted off and Jake did his best to observe the road, countered with incredulous glimpses at his brother. He was angry and confused at his own reactions. Levi had been unreliable, absent from familial obligation for so long, but *goddamn* if someone was going to try and kill his brother.

"Can't you ever do something the right way?" Jake asked. "The easy way? Without leaving a trail of shit to clean up. How concerned do I need to be about all this?"

"Everything'll be fine," Levi replied with his eyes closed.

"My ass," Jake muttered.

The orange and white lights of a '76 truck stop came into view, the only place open and busy along that stretch of highway.

"I'm going to stop and make a call," Jake said.

"To who?" a sleepy Levi replied.

"Who do you think? Rachel. Make sure everything is fine."

"Don't bring any of this up."

"You think I'm crazy?"

"Here, get me a few things," Levi replied as he dug into a pocket without opening his eyes, pulled a wad of bills, and offered them to Jake. "Cigarettes. You know what kind. A small bottle of whiskey. The good stuff. And some

Coors if they have it. And get some bandages, tape, some aspirin. That kind of stuff. Anything like that. And get yourself something."

Levi dozed off quickly. Jake accepted the money, a combination of bigger bills, and wanted to ask more questions, but there was no point in it. He put the offering into his jacket pocket and took the next exit from the highway for the truck stop.

A Peterbilt and Mack crossed paths in front of the wagon, one heading into the storm and the other heading for some respite. Jake waited his turn, then cruised past a row of idling rigs and around the side of the convenience store and parked.

He looked at his watch, then the rear-view mirror for any activity. It was nearly four in the morning, and the heaviness of the night and the weather weighed on him. He needed to stay alert and to think clearly. He parked the wagon, got out, and shut his door softly ajar.

Jake rounded to the back and open the door slowly to keep the warm air in and looked down on the old man. His eyes were closed, and his mouth was open. Jake put a hand down to his father's face and touched him on the cheek.

"Dad?"

The old man stirred.

"Huh?"

"Just checking on you. How are you feeling?"

"Oh?... Pretty good."

"OK, we're almost there. I'll be right back."

"Sounds good."

The Preacher offered no further response, and Jake let the heavy door close back softly and went back to the front of the car. He opened his driver's door and stuck his head in.

"Hey," he said to Levi.

Levi didn't respond, so Jake reached a hand in and pushed on his brother's shoulder again.

"Aaah!" Levi yelled.

"Don't forget Dad is in the back."

"Dammit!" Levi yelled as Jake let his door close and walked away. His arm throbbed where Jake touched him. It matched his pulse, beat by beat; dull, longing, uninterrupted. He needed relief, and he opened one eye just above the rim of his jacket and watched his brother go across the parking lot and disappear inside the store. Thank God his brother didn't push him to go inside. He wanted nothing more than to stay in the wagon's warmth, get something to dull the pain, and go to sleep. But dammit, the pain, and now he needed to pee.

Levi opened his door and dragged his legs out. He was stiff from the ride and the pain, and he seized and grimaced when he stood.

"Damn," he said to no one. He felt the warmth of his pulsating wound against the freezing cold of the air, then leaned in between the opening, unzipped, and drained himself.

He used the wagon as a crutch and relished the few seconds of relief. When he was through, he zipped up and slogged to the back of the wagon to check on the Preacher.

He opened the heavy door and looked in.

"Hey, Dad."

The old man didn't respond.

"Dad," Levi called louder.

The Preacher opened his eyes and peered up.

"Hello."

"How you feeling?"

"Ah, pretty good."

Levi studied the old man's face. They had some of the same features in the nose, the eyes. Most family members on the tree had brown eyes. They both had blue.

"My bible," the old man asked, and tried to work his hand free from the covers.

"What?"

"Where's... my bible?"

Levi peered around the back of the vehicle. There was no bible he could see. No books of any kind. He rummaged around a bit and spotted the syringes and the vials of morphine for the Preacher. He took his father's hand, felt the cold in it, and slid it back under the covers, then he lifted one syringe and vial and put them in his pocket.

"Kind of... thirsty," the Preacher muttered.

"Daddy, I don't see your bible right off. I'm sure it's here somewhere. Hang on and I'll get you a drink."

"Don't worry... about it. It'll show up. Always does."

Levi shut the door easily and glided along the side of the wagon to steady himself. He took the vial of morphine, stuck it unsteadily, and filled the syringe. His hands shook, but he'd done it before. Another lesson from 'Nam.

He plunged the needle into his thigh and pushed until it was empty. The wave of warmth rushed through his body. It was a release. The body, the mind. Let someone else take it from here. He laid his head against the top of the wagon.

Relief. Sweet relief. The bible. A drink.

"Hold on, Daddy," he spoke as he remembered, and he opened the passenger door to the backseat. Things were hazy now, but the pain melted away and the freedom washed over him. He dropped the empty vial and needle to the snow-covered pavement and thrashed around in the back seat for the

Preacher's bible and some water. Here were pamphlets on Leading a Christian Life, Immersive Baptism and Free Home Bible Studies, and then he spotted the well-creased bible on the floorboard under the edge of a blanket and reached down to get it.

He pushed a blanket out of the way and felt a movement along his hand and jerked back, hitting his head on the interior roof

What the hell?

He blinked his eyes and breathed to get his bearings. Something moved again, until he saw a shoe, then a leg, and he dragged the blanket until Benjamin poked his head out.

"Benji?"

"Uncle Levi? I'm sorry, Uncle Levi," Benji said. "I wanted to come."

"Oh, Jesus," Levi said. He felt faint, then buckled and fell backwards to the snow-covered concrete.

"Uncle Levi?" exclaimed Benji, and he scrambled out of the vehicle to his uncle on the ground.

"Uncle Levi!"

Levi moaned and Benji wondered what to do, so he ran to the store after his father.

Jake waited at the counter for the goods to be bagged up. Cigarettes, whiskey, beer, bandages; an assortment of items to help pay for the hard times of sin. The attendant took the cash, handed the change and receipt back, and Jake took his bag of goods out.

When he pushed the exit door, a bell clanked against the glass. He was thinking of the sound of the bell and how many times the clerk must hear it in a shift, and how annoying it would get day in and day out. He bit off the end of a Hershey bar and clenched it between his teeth. His hands were red from the cold as he held the bag and his chocolate. When he looked up and saw his son approach, his mouth dropped open and the chocolate spilled from his mouth.

"Benji!"

"Dad, it's Uncle Levi!"

"What did you do?"

"Uncle Levi's on the ground!"

Jake stifled his need to ask more questions and rushed back to the wagon. He sat the bag down on the cold ground and looked at his brother.

"Is he okay?" Benji asked.

Jake spied the empty vial and needle and knew what he'd done. He called out to his brother, then felt his pulse. When Levi moaned, Jake sat him up against the tire and pulled his jacket back to examine the bandage. He ran his hand around the back to check for the exit wound, then pulled out a canister, unscrewed the lid, and poured some of the water into it.

"He'll be alright," Jake said. "Take this to your grandpa."

Benji took the cup of water and jumped out of the door. He circled to the back and opened the heavy tailgate and slid himself in between it and the bumper and let it rest against his back.

"Hey, grandpa," he said. "It's me, Benji."

The old man smiled brightly.

"Benji."

It was hard for the boy to find the proper words for a last conversation. Jake was angry with his son, but his harshness gave way as he watched his son and his father through the sliding window over the bed of the wagon. He resigned himself to the situation and glanced at Levi.

"We'll be lucky if she hasn't called the law yet. Hopefully, she still thinks he's out in the woods."

There was no response from Levi.

"Should've just done this myself," Jake continued.

"Well, guess I better go see dad," Benji said to his grandfather, after offering some sips of water.

"Still playing… baseball?"

"Oh, yeah, I'm trying first base. Since I'm left-handed, like you."

"Good. Be alert. May get a bruise… or two… but it'll go away."

Benji nodded he understood and made sure the blanket was tight around his grandpa. He'd always had the old man, whether they were throwing a baseball in the front yard, sitting on the porch, and listening to the scolding of the mockingbirds and blue jays, or watching an old television show. Now, grandpa appeared shrunken and hollow, as if the light of his life was being moved to a faraway place.

Jake slapped Levi, pried his mouth open, and forced him to drink water. He slapped him several more times until he took more in.

"Get it down," Jake told him.

Levi moaned and accepted the water that coughed its way down his mouth. The rest sloshed across his cheeks and shirt, but Jake kept pouring.

"Gotta go now," Benji said to the Preacher.

"Ok," the Preacher nodded, and blinked his eyes. "See you… later."

Benji nodded back and carefully shut the door over his grandfather, then hurried back with the cup.

"He drank a little."

Jake took the cup and tossed the remaining water to the ground, then bent over and picked up Levi under an arm. He grabbed Levi by his belt with his other hand and felt the hard handle of the gun and pulled it out. He knew Levi had his experience with guns from the war, but this didn't add up. Levi wasn't the type of criminal that carried a gun, at least as much as he knew his brother. He opened the glove compartment and put the gun away, then finished hoisting Levi up and plopped him back into his seat.

"Get in," Jake called to his son.

"Is Uncle Levi going to die?" he asked his father.

"Not from this," he replied. "Did your uncle help you get in here?"

"No, Dad, I swear, he didn't do anything. I wanted to go."

Jake didn't know what else to add or ask. This was a typical set of outcomes with his brother. Where his brother went, chaos and conflict followed. Levi had somehow gotten himself shot instead of what should've been a typical furlough, the Preacher was getting closer to heaven in the back of the wagon, the weather was terrible, and now his son had hidden himself away in full defiance and gotten into the mix. There was no time to return, and the issue now was how to deal with his wife.

"Dammit, Benji!" was all he could think to say.

"Please don't be mad, Dad."

"Well, there is no time and no way to turn back," Jake replied.

"I'm sorry, Dad. I'll keep quiet. I promise."

"Did you hear everything we've been talking about?" Jake asked.

"Yes."

Jake sighed and looked at his watch for the time.

"I didn't hear anything new, Dad. You always said Uncle Levi was trouble."

Jake's eyes grew wide, and he looked toward his brother for a reaction, but there was none.

"Dad?" asked Benji.

"Yeah?"

"I have to pee."

"Of course you do. Come on then," Jake replied. "Need to call your mother, anyway."

The sky continued its torrent of snowfall as Jake and Benji shuffled back into the truck stop. The neon lights beckoned to another large truck, pulling a long load of hidden contents behind it.

"Shit," Jake exclaimed, almost falling near the payphone hanging at the corner of the store. Jake fed dimes into the phone and dialed the house number. It rang several times before his wife finally picked up.

"Hello?" Rachel said.

"I've got Benji."

"What? Oh, Jesus Christ. What time is it?"

"He snuck into the back. I didn't know, didn't see him."

"I fell asleep," she sighed. "Oh my God, I had no idea. Figured he had come in. You know how stubborn he is. Put him on the phone."

Jake handed the phone to his son with a stern look.

"Momma?"

"Benjamin, what do you think you are doing?"

"I'm sorry, Momma. I...I...wanted to go. I tried to tell you."

She breathed a heavy sigh.

"Well, there's nothing we can do now, but you and I are going to have a talk when you get home. Now, put your daddy back on the phone."

He sheepishly handed the phone back to Jake.

"I'm going to tear him a new one when he gets home," Rachel said to Jake.

"Well, everything's fine now," Jake replied, looking at his son. "No use worrying."

"Right," she replied. "You're with your brother and our son out in a storm with your dying father."

Another heavy sigh, and Jake looked stern at his son for the trouble he'd caused and mouthed the word *thanks*.

"Alright," she replied. "I shouldn't have said all that. I'm tired. I'm going back to bed while the baby's asleep. Is there anything else I need to know? Any further surprises?"

"No, nothing at all. We'll be fine. You go back to bed."

"Okay. Love you."

"You, too."

Jake hung the phone up and looked at Benji. He didn't like to deceive his wife. His brother's condition and the gun gave him pause, but there was no good reason to tell her anything further and get her concerned.

"Let's go pee," he said to Benji, who followed him into the store.

The boy was cheerful at the outcome, but he was smart enough not to share any look of content with his dad. They did their business in the stalls and said nothing further to each other on the way to the car or as they got back in. Jake glanced at his dozing brother, then shifted the wagon into reverse.

Benji watched as the truck stop faded into the distance. He observed his father and his uncle from the back, his father with one hand across the top of the wheel, slouched toward his door, eyes locked on the road ahead. His uncle had his head on his chest, slumped over with his hands in his lap, one shoulder higher than the other. Benji imagined how different his father and uncle were, and yet he noticed some similarities. The way they smiled and laughed and talked, the same as grandpa.

The bond between the men was the old man in the back. Benji looked back through the sliding glass window at his grandpa, quiet and unmoved, his face occasionally lit by the lights over the highway, then he gazed out his own window. The flakes appeared like magic from the darkness of the sky, and

Benji tried to track one from the many and follow the journey as long as he could. He again looked over the back seat through the sliding glass at his grandpa, then relaxed into his seat, proud of his success. He was where he wanted to be.

He didn't like the feeling of his parents being upset with him, but he knew it would pass. This was the Preacher. This was his grandpa, and though he didn't understand everything, he knew grandpa would. He turned his attention back to his uncle, snoring a deep slumber.

"Should we wake him up?" Benji asked about his uncle.

"No," Jake replied. "He's breathing. Let him sleep. Be easier for all of us."

PONTIUS RETURNS

The hours passed quietly at home for the sheriff. One thing an overnight snow promised was less criminal activity. There might be a car ditched off an icy road or a wandering homeless boozer frozen to ice, but most thieves and lowlifes preferred not to prowl around in the cold. Crime was manageable enough to keep a skeleton crew patrolling the night shift and his own activities dedicated to the day.

The sheriff often woke immediately. He never lay in the dark in his bed with his own thoughts. It was good genes to have for a lawman and he faced each day with the same expectation of hell and bounty to come. He was a special breed, an early riser since the Marines trained him to survive Korea, survive losing a son, and to run a jail by fear alone.

The sheriff was in a satisfactory mood driving to the office. The morning represented some needed changes. Out with the old, and in with the new. A new year was coming, and he would rejoice in his way and be glad in it. It was still dark, when he thought on another lowlife to use as a middleman. The kid that bunked with Levi was malleable; slow and unmoored to anyone or anything. There were plenty of sad sacks like the kid that couldn't cope with life. The sheriff would offer an expectation, and let the kid trade his services for jail time and keep a few bucks, too. If the kid couldn't muster that, well, he wasn't worth tits on a boar. It'd be time to take out the trash and join Levi Johnson.

The sheriff radioed overnight patrol for their reports and cruised at a leisurely rate. His big green rig broke the quiet as he turned into the jail lot and reversed into his parking spot. He cut the radio, the wipers, the engine, then stepped out and down, and shut the door with one hand without locking it. He whistled and kept his other hand warm around the hot mug of joe. The sheriff stared at the vacant spot where Levi's truck usually sat and felt a rush of satisfaction. It was an early gift. A well-played part. Yes, the holidays were looking good.

He reached the side door to his office, pulled on his chain at his waistband, and stuck a bulky bronze key in the lock. He twisted until the frozen pins inside clicked and the door cracked open. The door shut behind him and he watched his chilly breath dissipate in the air and knew the staff had followed orders and not turned the thermostat up. It was the first sign of instilled discipline. He was proud of his ability to command the necessary respect without being present.

He was thinking about plans next week when the first thing that caught his attention was the placement of papers on his desk. Something was amiss. His mind cascaded through the logic of expectations. His training kicked in and he instinctively moved a hand toward his holster. He took two strides to the other side of the desk and scanned the pieces of the broken mug. He pulled his gun and opened the inner door.

The hallways were clear. The door to the holding cells were shut tight, but then a sound. A small, muffled murmur of noise. He moved in a steady, rhythmic stride to the janitor's closet, his gun at the ready. He cracked the mop with a kick, turned a knob, and opened the door. Burns, tied and gagged, peered wide-eyed back at him. The sight of Burns with his shiny dark shoes and his creased pants and starched shirt all wrapped up tight on the floor in such a helpless manner was a shock and an absurdity.

Trouble.

Burns mumbled through the gag in his mouth, and the blood left the sheriff's face and rushed toward his enlarged eyes. He moved quickly from Burns back to his office and to the desk and the drawers and then to the safe, where he dialed the code in quickly and spun it open. Despite the temperature in the room, a bead of sweat popped free on his forehead and he placed a hand almost involuntarily on the desk to steady himself.

The safe was empty. He blinked. It was still empty. This needed immediate triage. A quick regain of his territory. It meant urgency and the strong possibility of killing someone. It was that or losing pride and place, a colossal embarrassment. A loss of his credibility. It meant living with scandal.

"Son of a bitch," he muttered, almost whispered, in an agonizing pitch meant for no one. "Was it Levi Johnson?"

Burns mumbled from the other room and the sheriff placed his hand inside the open drawers and the shelves of the safe and brushed around to feel the cold emptiness and confirm this new reality.

Then another discomfort hit him. Not only had the bastard taken the money, but he'd also taken the ledger. The ledger was the sheriff's black book, his accounting of who moved what and how much in order to milk the extra revenue and not get cheated by the cheaters.

He stared for several seconds at the emptiness to ensure his brain of this reality. His pride burned, and it fueled the anger inside of him. He breathed deeply with shock and anger until the thrill of hunting a man down churned in him and changed his anger to anticipation. He felt a fresh surge of energy. He'd cultivated a reputation, and this little bastard Levi Johnson would become an opportunity yet again.

"Mm mph, mph," Burns mumbled through the tape on his mouth, and the sheriff went back to the janitor's closet. He'd never seen one of his own deputies tied up. Who dared do that to one of his men?

The sheriff's eyes moistened in anticipation as he hatched a plan of recovery. If he could find Levi Johnson in time, he might get the money back. He'd burn the ledger. That was a mistake. He'd put a bullet in the bastard himself. That was another mistake.

The sheriff bent over and ripped the piece of tape from Burn's mouth. Burns spit a ball of cloth out and gasped.

"How did you let this happen?" he asked Burns.

Burns enjoyed breathing the cold air, and the sheriff strolled away, not waiting for an answer.

"Not sure who it was," Burns called out. "I heard a noise, came in, and it was lights out."

Burns paused and reflected. This was important. Whatever came out, there was no taking it back.

"Could've been Johnson," Burns added. "I came from the cells. Had to be someone from outside."

The sheriff came back and looked at Burns in anger. "And you let him get the drop on you?"

Burns did not answer, and the sheriff went back to his office and looked out at the empty parking spots and the sky outside. Burns ripped the tape and waited for the story to take hold with each second that passed. This was the point of impact. Either Burns was to be believed, or the sheriff would finish him.

"That's the problem with these lowlifes," the sheriff finally replied, with a change in his tone. "They do something like this, you gotta go set things right. They got no respect for anything. No guiding compass. Nothing sacred."

"Should I call it in?" Burns asked, still bound to the pipes. He dared not to ask the sheriff for help, though his body ached from being stuck in the same position.

The sheriff returned to Burns and pulled a knife from his belt. He flicked it open, walked over, and bent over Burns. Burns tightened up.

"Are you crazy, Burns? Can you picture how this looks right now? The barrel of shit that would come down on me. On us! How the hell did you let this happen?"

The knife came closer, and Burns jerked his eyes from the sheriff to the blade. It would take just a moment, a split second, to add to the crime at hand and blame it all on Levi Johnson. Instead, the sheriff stuck the knife between the bonds and cut Burns loose with quick swipes, then he rose and went back to his office and unlocked the gun cabinet with his tangle of keys.

"We keep complete radio silence," the sheriff instructed. "Not a Goddamned word until I have that sonofabitch in the bed of my truck."

Burns breathed a sigh of relief and rubbed the knot on his head and the stiffness of his neck. The sheriff selected a sawed-off shotgun with two barrels, then filled his pockets with shells. He loaded several shells into the chamber and pumped it ready.

Burns finished removing the rest of the tape and worked to rub the life back into his bones. He rose to his knees with some trouble, then walked back into the sheriff's office. The sheriff observed him with disgust.

"We'll talk about this later," the sheriff said. "Get this cleaned up like it never happened. Is that understood?"

The sheriff singed a hole in Burn's soul with his stare, and Burns nodded he understood. The sheriff exited his office into the cold dark morning, his gait quicker than usual and the shotgun at his side. Burns looked around the floor and at the empty safe. He was in it now, and he would have to play his part until Levi Johnson was dead.

Burns eyed the pieces of the broken mug scattered on the floor.

"Shit," Burns muttered to himself. "That was my favorite cup."

FOG OF MEMORIES

Jake widened his eyes and stretched his mouth to combat fatigue. Benji slept in the backseat while Levi slumbered with his chin on his chest and his head rolling back and forth. His mouth was open a half clam, just wide enough for the air to throttle in and out with a ruckus.

With the sky letting loose in thicker waves, he needed all the concentration he could muster and kept to the slushy course left in front of him by other drivers. When those tracks faded away, he relied on the headlights and the wipers to remain steady and true for the endless switchbacks and saw-toothed progress.

Benjamin woke and leaned forward over the seat and viewed the road from between his father and uncle. The conditions were treacherous, yet the boy had no notion of the danger. They were on a mission, and he was part of the team. His finger followed a loose tan thread until it ended near his uncle's wrapped-up shoulder. He let his finger continue to draw an invisible trace in the fabric until he squished too hard into the shoulder and woke his uncle.

Levi looked at his nephew out of the corner of his eye.

"What are you doing?" he asked Benji.

"Is this where you got shot?"

Levi grunted a yes and hoped that would be the end.

"Where did you get your tattoos?"

Levi cleared his throat.

"Here and there," he answered, again hoping the boy would let him sleep.

"Dad said they were jailhouse tattoos."

"Maybe so," Levi replied after a bit. "Doesn't matter."

Benji was most interested in the one on his uncle's neck, a dragonfly about three inches tall, immaculately drawn in emerald, green, and blue.

"What about this one?" Benji asked, and poked again.

Levi grunted again at the interruption.

"Will you let me be if I tell ya?"

The boy didn't answer, and Levi sighed.

"That's for a girl I used to know, to cover up a scar there. Another story. Another time."

Levi adjusted his neck for comfort and pulled on his collar to cover the symbol. He hoped his nephew would ask no further questions.

"I might get a tattoo," Benji added. "But it'd have to be like this one. I like the colors. I don't like the other ones. They look kind of plain."

"Let's change the subject," interjected Jake.

Levi raised his head and sat up in his seat with a groan, fished around for his cigarettes and cracked the window. Jake tossed over the brown paper bag and Levi felt the contents inside without looking. He felt for the familiar size of a pint of whiskey, took it, undid the cap, and swallowed down an ample portion.

"Take it easy," Jake said.

"If you get a tattoo," Levi continued, clearing his voice of the booze backwash, "make sure you can cover it. Lots of people don't like 'em."

Jake observed Levi with both pity and scorn. Time had taken its toll. Benji looked closer at the bloodstain on the bandages, curious to ask more questions. Jake spied his son in the rearview mirror and anticipated his interest.

"I thought you said you were going to be quiet and stay out of the way," Jake chided Benji. The boy sat back in his seat, gazed through the sliding glass at his grandpa, then put his eyes to his own window.

Another mile marker drifted by in the lights. The station wagon bounced along the highway, and the wipers swung for visibility. Jake turned the dial to another station. Country and bluegrass faded in and out, and the next rotation offered old time religion and faded love songs.

"Shit," Jake said. "Guess they expect everyone to be asleep in bed."

Levi assessed the supply of cigarettes he had, then tried to limit his intake to every ten miles. Then it became the next city sign, or if he saw a red Chevy. Benji gave up asking any more questions and was soon asleep with the hum and rocking of the vehicle. Jake remained focused on staying on the road and getting to the mountain, and Levi kept mostly quiet in a stupor of pain and self-medication. He moved just enough to take another swig of whiskey, an inhale of smoke, then exhaled an elixir of fumes.

Jake tried the radio again, turning the knob until it played a local station where the man talked in the local pro-nunc-i-a-shun about the weather, the high school football team, and the sale of toolboxes at the hardware store. The talk of toolboxes led both to recall the heavy, full toolbox the Preacher brought home once. He bought them off an air force man getting ready to move to Biloxi, and the Preacher figured if Levi could find something to keep his hands occupied, the rest of him would follow. But the plan didn't take, and Levi couldn't even remember how much he had pawned them for and what he spent the money on.

Jake remembered more of the details, and how Levi had pawned the tools for a couple of quarter bags of weed. When his dad asked about them, Levi was defiant. Jake hated Levi for it, and the logic he used to go his own way.

"You gave em to me," Levi said. *"I can do what I want with them."*

"I didn't give them to you to sell," his father pleaded. *"I gave them to you to develop some skills, a work ethic. Idle time is when the devil gets you."*

The weight of the memories set heavy upon each of them, and the brothers rode for miles more with nothing but the drone of the radio. The front windows remain cracked to filter the cigarette smoke out, and the heater blew good and hot.

"I remember when Daddy ran off the interstate once," said Levi, breaking the silence between them. "Must have been weather like this. I don't know why we weren't with him. Anyway, he was near Nashville. Said he fell asleep and skidded right off the interstate into the median. Some good Samaritan came along, those were Dad's words, and pulled him out. I could see the fear in his eyes when he told the story. I don't think he thought he was coming home. Said it was an angel that saved him. Swore on it. The man appeared out of nowhere, in the dead of night, and then just like that, the man was gone."

Jake took the story in and wondered why he'd never heard it straight from the Preacher.

"Do you remember any of his sermons?" Jake replied. "I counted out one day that we must've sat through over 2,000 of them, but I can only remember bits and pieces. A few sayings here and there. I ask myself, how is that possible? I remember more about the places and the people, but how can I not remember more of what he was saying?"

"It all starts running together," Levi offered. "Wasn't preaching for us, anyway. We were just the help."

"Whatever," Jake replied.

"I tell you what I remember. Little things, like the man always snoring during Daddy's sermon."

"You mean the man in Greenville," Jake added correctly.

"Every time that man came," Levi went on, "he slept, and Daddy would work him right into the lesson."

Don't get me wrong, brothers and sisters, I do my best not to bore you with the Word of God.

The Preacher walked slowly and quietly and stood near the sleeping man.

Brothers and sisters, don't catch yourself sleeping at the chosen hour. You know the time I'm talking about. When the Lord returns... like a thief in the night.

"No one ever told that old geezer," Levi continued. "He'd wake up when the singing started and join right in. It annoyed Daddy, but I think the people kept coming for that little bit of extra entertainment."

"Maybe I shouldn't mention this, but I once walked in on Daddy and Mrs. Lynch," Jake said to his brother. "You remember her?"

"The widow who lived in Macon?"

"Yeah," answered Jake, and he took a quick glance at his brother.

Levi reflected on events that somehow got by him and took a drag from his cigarette. "Here all this time, I thought he was taking a nap."

Levi tried to turn to look back toward the Preacher but could barely manage.

"You sneaky little… that explains why we stayed over there so much."

"She could cook, too," Jake added. "Venison steak, mashed potatoes. Kind of thought Daddy would end up staying there and settling down. Wouldn't have been so bad."

"There was another guy out there in that town," Levi added. "He'd bring Daddy a skinned raccoon, and he'd pass the coon on to Mrs. Lynch. What was his name? Simpson, I think."

"Yeah," Jake replied, "another old buzzard. Brother Simpson."

"He took me hunting one time. Had those coon hounds with him. That was the first time I ever shot a gun. His dogs chased a raccoon up a tree, and he handed me the gun and let me shoot. It knocked me on my ass, but I think I shot its nose off. It wobbled and stretched, then it hit about every branch on the way down."

Levi paused for another drag of his cigarette, and memories of other events.

"He used to leave his handkerchief hanging out of his pocket all the time. When he blew his nose, it was like a trumpet. I couldn't keep from laughing. It'd make Daddy mad. Anyways, I was more interested in the Hatman girl."

"Oh, I know what you're sayin," Jake replied.

"Do you?"

"Yeah. I always liked Rebecca."

"I always liked Linda," Levi replied. "First time I ever saw a set."

The brothers looked at each other.

"I heard Linda ran off with someone," Jake added. "Left the family, the farm, everything. Just disappeared."

"Can't say I blame her. They used to work that farm from sunup until sundown. That's how we ended up in the barn."

Levi glanced a knowing twinkle at Jake.

"What about the old blind lady?" Jake asked.

"Ms. Tilley?" Levi replied. "Couldn't forget her. She was built like a tailback. Squat, thick. I was always afraid that if she tripped, she'd keep on rolling."

Levi forgot his pain and felt the warmth of the vehicle and the memory.

"You know, when Daddy had us serve the Lord's supper, she'd put her hand in a certain way and put her fingers together so you could put the little cup right in it. I also picked her up a bunch of times. Daddy would give me the keys, told me to go get her in the wagon, so she didn't have to walk in the road. Figured it was only a couple blocks, I'd be alright."

"One time I got there, knocked on the door, and she hollered for me to come in. I went on in and I looked down the hallway and there she was, sitting right on the pot, her pantyhose wrapped around her knees, and finishing her business. Of course, she couldn't see that I could see, so I slowly inched my way back out and knocked on the door like I hadn't come in yet. That's one time I wished it was me that was blind."

Jake looked at his brother and smiled at the memory.

"Maybe you forgot about the other lady we used to see. The big one."

"Who?"

"The big lady. Down by Chickasaw. Used to come in late and sit in the back, but then she moved up a row each week until she was taking up the front and wanted to be baptized. You remember?"

Levi thought for a moment and rubbed an eye with his thumb before he moved in his seat and recalled an event.

"I almost forgot about that. She almost drowned Daddy. He dunked her in the lake and couldn't pull her up."

"We had to jump in and help Daddy bring her back up," Jake added. "Daddy didn't make fun of people, but I remember him saying, 'That lady was carrying a lot of sin.'"

The brothers smiled at the memory and Levi put a hand to his shoulder and side and stretched a bit. Jake twisted the knob on the radio to see about a different station, this one playing an old George Jones song.

"You never talk much about the army," Jake asked.

Levi grunted.

"Why would I do that?"

"No stories to share?" Jake asked. "Come on, gotta be something worth mentioning."

Levi took a long, slow draw of his smoke before he flicked the bud out the window.

"Should've never been made to go."

"What? You're gonna blame Daddy for that?"

"I didn't really have a choice."

"Based on… your record of wonderful decisions," Jake jested.

Jake glanced in the rearview mirror, then twisted around to check on any movement from their father or Benji.

"I see Pops got to you pretty good," Levi retorted.

"Not sure what that means. Last time I checked, you had plenty of choices with Daddy paying the bills."

"Whatever," Levi replied with a grimace as the pain in his shoulder throbbed.

"You know, you've always had a messed-up way of looking at things," Jake continued. "Here's the old man dying in the back, working until the day he couldn't, and you think of yourself. You drew the short end of the stick."

Jake gripped the steering wheel and tried to quell a rising anger.

"Benji?" Jake called without looking in the back.

The boy stirred and moved the cover from his face.

"Check on grandpa."

The boy sat up and slid the small window open and looked into the bed at his grandpa.

"I think he's asleep," then added quietly, "and he may have pooped."

Maybe it wasn't just what Levi said, but how sure he was of what he said. Jake tapped on the steering wheel and took a few breaths to calm himself down and stop the cascade of memories. Levi put a hand up near his shoulder, curious to feel the heat, the sensation of the throb.

"That's always been the problem," Jake continued. "You're my brother, but the asshole part is always just under the skin."

"All high and mighty," Levi answered in a slow drawn-out parsing of the words.

Benji listened wide-eyed from the back.

"You're kidding, right?" Jake guffawed. "I always had to make up for your shit. The calls in the middle of the night. Daddy having to go to the jail to visit your sorry ass. Listening to you running your mouth and complaining after you steal cars or flowers or whatever. Even pawning off mother's ring? Oh yeah, I knew about that. I got it back, you dumb ass."

Jake breathed and took a pause.

"Should've kept your sorry ass in jail."

The brothers sat in silence as another mile passed and the weather kept a somber pallor over them.

"You asked me about the war," Levi offered. "I'll tell you what it is. It's being somewhere you don't want to be. Smelling the fear on the guy next to you. He tries to tell you his girlfriend's name, but you don't want to know. He tells you things he's never told anyone. Then suddenly, he's gone. And you try to forget him. Forget all of it. It just clings to you, and you pretend everything's ok. Everything has a reason, or no reason at all."

"Then there's God, and you wonder what the hell? What am I doing out here? People will give you some line to have faith, have more faith, give it up to God, until you realize... nobody really knows anything. They're making shit up."

Levi looked off into the distance, out the window.

"I wanted to talk to Pops about it, but he wouldn't understand."

"Dad?" Benji interrupted.

"What?" Jake replied.

"I have a question."

"Yeah?"

"What happens when we die?"

"See the shit you started," Jake said to Levi.

The brothers looked at each other.

"Your grandpa would tell you you'll see Jesus," Levi offered.

Benji thought on the answer. Jake looked at his son in the rearview mirror, then back to the road ahead. The brothers sat silent, mulling over their own thoughts and emotions, as they passed a sign that advertised cheeseburgers at the next stop.

"You see that?" Levi nodded toward the sign. "If there is a God, he's probably sitting out there right now, eating a cheeseburger, looking around, wondering what the hell have we done."

Benji listened to his uncle and looked at his father for a response.

"Try not to sell any more of your crazy shit to my son," Jake said. "Look for the turnoff."

GONE, BUT NOT FORGOTTEN

The elevator doors slid open, and Sheriff Price disembarked in a quick steady cadence. With his face creased tight and his mouth pursed closed, he kept a hand resting on his belt near the butt of his gun and let the other arm swing loose. He scanned the numbers on the wall and along each room for the right set.

This one.

He moved directly to the room of the Preacher, paused, and slid his hand to his weapon. He stuck his head in, then the rest of him followed.

Empty.

The bed lay cleaned and prepped for the next patient, as if no one had ever been there. Not a trace. He made his way to the nurse's station, where an older black nurse in a starched white uniform looked up at him over her glasses.

"What happened with the patient in room 301?" the sheriff asked.

"The Preacher?" she replied and pulled out her patient register. She flipped through the records and ran a finger down a page.

"Checked out last night," she continued. "Well, that is a bit strange."

"What is it?"

"He wasn't scheduled for release."

The nurse dropped her voice.

"Unless he passed."

"Well, go find out," the sheriff ordered.

The nurse gazed at the sheriff over her glasses and backed up in her chair.

"Uh, let me see if I can find the nurse from that shift. If she is still around."

As she left, his fingers tapped impatiently on the counter. He squeezed the handle of his holstered gun out of habit. The clock ticked on, and every second meant the problem getting beyond his reach. All he needed was a lead, a confirmation of his suspicions.

He peered past the nurse station to the long window and the snow falling heavy. It could be anytime of the day with the sun blotted out. He looked at his watch and then down one end of the hallway and missed seeing the one person who knew something. The nurse who'd assisted Levi and Jacob saw the sheriff first and she quickly scurried into a patient's room and took a heavy breath.

He glanced back to the clock on the wall, greedy to hunt the problem down. The muscles in his jaw clenched as he imagined the whole thing. The sheriff made it his business to assess every scenario, to be ahead of the game and know people in the town and where they'd come from, where they worked, and where they drank. He remembered the Preacher first coming into town and his visits to the jail that he didn't want, and then the sheriff remembered a place he'd heard mentioned before.

"I'm from the land between the lakes," the Preacher had said. "Not much there anymore except memories."

That was it.

God-damn, he thought to himself. *God-dammit!*

The nurse from the station returned.

"Well, the patient is not in the morgue," she offered. "It's a little unusual. I'll have to run this one down."

The sheriff turned on his heels without a word. It was all clear to him.

"Sheriff?" she called after him.

I'll hang him to a tree.

This was bad. The mountain, the area he was familiar with, was across the state line and it was a goddamned blizzard. He had no time for talk. He'd deal with the hospital later. He'd chew a new hole into Burn's ass for letting this happen. He'd visit with the Curry boys for double-crossing him. There'd be some hell to pay from all of them. Right now, his mind and body surged with anticipation.

He had a mission to complete.

CLOSER TO THEE

With the sun fighting a losing battle, Jake kept the headlights on and the wagon churned through the thick globs of dirty snow. He rested his head against his hand and drove with the other, his eyes darting between the bouncing gauges on his dashboard and the road. His thoughts weighed heavy and were aggravated by the lack of sleep. He read a billboard for Mountain Dew, the hillbilly choice of pop, and then observed the headlights from the other direction flash their brights. He dimmed his in response and recalled the time an owl flew into the headlights, and the Preacher and the boys stopped on the side of the road and tried to find the wounded bird.

The Preacher would also pick up the occasional hitchhikers, take them as far as they were already travelling, and invite them to a service. If the person didn't ask for any money, the Preacher would often give them a couple of bucks for a meal or two. If they asked for something, the Preacher would usually claim he had two boys to raise. Anytime the boys thought they knew who would get money and who wouldn't, the Preacher would surprise them.

"Many of these folks have been eaten up and spit out," he told the boys. "I don't want to add to their iniquities. Neither do I want to be foolish with our limited funds. I can usually tell within a matter of seconds. Least we can do is spend a bit of time and remind them of the love of God."

"Don't you think some of these fellas are dangerous, Daddy?" Levi asked. "You don't know where they've been. They could've been an escape criminal or something."

"I put on the whole armor of God," the Preacher replied. "That's all we need to protect ourselves and feed the flock. Now, this is a man's world, and being a man is hard to do and some men can't live with the expectations that come with that. Sometimes they revert to their natural ways of being out in the wild. They turn to gambling or drinking or something else to fill what's missing. Little do they know. All they really need, they already have."

Jake remembered how his father often talked in riddles.

"Now, if you see a woman out here by herself, someone has done something awful bad. Probably a man. It just isn't natural. A woman wants to nest, to make a home. Being out here on the road. Can't be anything good about it. Everyone wants a place called home."

Jake would look at his brother when the Preacher would talk about such things, and Levi would often shake his head like the Preacher was crazy and lean over and whisper to his brother, *where's our home.*

"Where are we?" Levi asked. "What time is it?"

"We're close. About eight in the morning. Running behind."

"How close is close?"

"Look around. You don't remember?"

Levi gazed out the windows in various directions. He'd not been near the homestead in years. The pain in his body clogged his memory as he searched for a familiar sign or landmark. He scooted up in his seat and drained the last few drops of whiskey, then opened his jacket and shirt to look over the angry wound. The morphine he'd clipped from his dad's supply had knocked him out good, but the pain came on in ebbs and flows.

"Are you gonna make it?"

Levi didn't answer.

"You won't be any good to me dead."

"I'll be fine," Levi replied.

"Then keep an eye out for the turn. Might not even be a road anymore."

Jake occasionally checked the rearview mirror for any other vehicles coming up from behind, and any movement of the Preacher, but the road was mostly theirs alone and the Preacher appeared to be resting comfortably.

They passed a speed limit sign, a county line sign, then a historic marker for the place where a famous country singer died. It was familiar territory, snapshots of youthful travels with the Preacher.

There were no signs that trouble was in pursuit.

BROAD IS THE WAY

Blizzard conditions swept across the region and weather reports gave no indication of it letting down. The sheriff checked his scanner and radio and pushed the Hulk faster than he should have given the conditions of the road. He had to cut time, and without good weather and a hot mug of coffee, the sheriff's mood was cured only by the thought of a successful capture and kill.

He'd have his story straight by the time he returned to the jail. His ace in the hole was Burns. Burns was on duty. Burns knew the Preacher and Levi. If it came to it, Burns would take the heat for this mess. The money and the ledger were what he wanted, and Levi's head on the wall like a trophy. No one got the better of him. He knew what needed to be done.

The heat blasted full, but it was still cold, and he gripped the steering wheel with gloved hands. *Cold like Korea*, he thought to himself.

He'd have it all figured out by the time he got to the land between the lakes. That was where the home mountain was, what the locals always called it, in the border area along the Tennessee and Kentucky line. The sheriff had enough knowledge of the region to know how to get there and get things done with no local law enforcement getting involved. But it had to be fast, a quick get in and get out, and damn this weather.

The sheriff dealt with people from the area all the time. Hillbillies, he called them, yet they knew everything there was to live off the land whether they grew corn, tobacco, moonshine, or marijuana. Many of them had ventured over to Boone when a coal mine fouled the water and bought the land for pennies on the dollar, a part of eminent domain procedures that saw the feds and the company work together to empty the land of its people.

That's how the sheriff learned who was who. He kept tabs on who came through and who blended in, and it gave him the ability to make a name for himself. That was the silver lining. More people meant more crime and more opportunities for growth. The order of things suited him. He liked to be in charge. He thought he could have done more in the military. Maybe make a career and pension if not for the bureaucracy. Not enough leadership. Too many gray areas. He could be king of his own country in Boone. The thoughts gave him a sense of pride, a momentary joy, but they spoiled on the reality of Levi Johnson.

The sheriff gripped and cracked his knuckles against the cold. Johnson represented everything gone wrong in the world. The sheriff's own boy had volunteered for Vietnam, leadership material the recruiters had called him, only to come back in a box, while someone like Mr. Big Shot, a delinquent and lawbreaker, had to be conscripted in and lived.

It wasn't right.

And to think this waste had a father who was a preacher, who'd come in and pray with his criminal son, while his boy was cold in the ground.

It wasn't right.

The sheriff wouldn't have it. He'd set things right. He'd return things to a proper order.

END OF THE ROAD

I have fought the good fight.

The billboards and signs that beckoned travelers competed to be seen against the current of wind and snow. Off in the distance were the small homes and farms and old wooden fences that crisscrossed across large open fields, seen now mostly by the Christmas lights strung up and the occasional spots of John Deere green or brick red. There'd been no traffic on the road for a few miles, and Levi, being of no assistance, had returned to the land of dreams. Jake made out a familiar rusted and bent sign for a local tractor supply and remembered it as the marker for the right junction.

I have finished the course.

The road that turned and ran up the mountain was non-distinct from the rest, except for the sign and the heavy vegetation. It was a forgotten place because of the steep ravines and the sharp elevation. Farming was easier down below and vehicles only came up the road if they were lost, or if teenagers looked for a remote place to do what teenagers do. The occasional logging trucks made their way up the mountain to clear various plots and parcels, but not in inclement weather and, from all appearances, not for some time. The land had been left to nature after the Preacher and the rest of the kinfolk died or departed.

I have kept the faith.

Snow had filled the dirt ruts and concealed the true condition of the road. Jake drove the wagon over and through what he could see, and the vehicle rocked back and forth and spun its tires across each ancient dip and pothole. He stopped at a pole fence strung haphazardly across the way, with a sign hanging on at an angle sporting a few bullet holes, and the faded words *Keep Out*.

Jake observed the surroundings. The limbs of the forest balanced stacks of snow while the groundcover did its best to poke through. The remaining journey climbed higher through the woods, and he knew the wagon was incapable of conquering the entire rise. Jake kept the car running in park, reached over and took one of his brother's cigarettes, lit it, and took a deep drag. He then reached over, opened the glove box, and removed the gun.

The trip had taken longer than normal due to the weather, but they'd made it. If they could carry the Preacher up the rest of the way, they'd use timber from the old house and get a fire going. They could make it together for a couple of days and let nature take its course in familiar surroundings. If the Preacher appeared in pain, he'd use the morphine.

He got out to face the cold and the wind and put the gun in his coat pocket. The snow whipped against him, and he let the gusts take his half-smoked cigarette as he bent forward to face it and get to the back of the wagon. He opened the back and stood between the tailgate and the Preacher to block the cold. When he looked down over his father, the Preacher's eyes were open to slits and his mouth was agape.

Jake paused for a few seconds before the realization set in. His will and wishes fought with the reality of the situation. He put a hand down to touch his father, to feel for life.

"Dad?"

He touched his father lightly on the shoulder, across his head, and along his cheek, but the Preacher did not stir.

"Dad?" he called again.

Jake bent down close and put his ear to his father's nose and mouth, but there was nothing.

The Preacher had passed.

The snow gathered on Jake's back and a few flakes fell along the Preacher's face. Jake's eyes teared and he placed his forehead to his father's.

"Did the best I could, Dad," he said to him. "But you're home now."

They hadn't made it. There would be no more last visit to the old homestead. They had been so close. He wondered if he should have stopped, wondered if the Preacher had died in pain, whether he should have given him the morphine, and then the usual anger with Levi rose.

Jake backed away and quietly shut the door. He left the wagon and trudged toward the fence that blocked the road. He bent down and wedged himself in between the strands of wire, then walked away into the woods.

FROM THE MOUTH OF BABES

When Benji awoke, the engine was running, and the wipers did their best against the snow gathered across the windshield. His father was gone, and Uncle Levi lay head back with his nose and mouth pointing toward the roof of the wagon. Benji's side window was thick with ice, and when he tried to roll it down, it wouldn't budge. He scurried to the sliding window behind him, opened it, and looked in on the Preacher.

"Grandpa?"

There was no answer, and Benji turned to his door and pushed against it until it opened. His boots sunk inches into the snow, and he tried to look in every direction for his father.

"Dad!" he hollered across the woods, but there was no answer and no sign of him.

Levi awoke with a jolt, gained his bearings, and rubbed his eyes. He moaned when he lifted his arm. The stiffness had set in, and the wound balked at being stretched. He felt nauseous and quickly opened his door to puke into the fresh snow.

Benji came around the wagon to stand beside Levi as his uncle spit the last bit of remnants from his mouth.

"What is it?" Levi asked.

"I don't know where Dad is," Benji told him, then his voice broke. "And I think you better check on Grandpa."

Levi looked up at his nephew and saw the hurt in his eyes. He rose and braced himself against the wagon and walked to the back, then opened the door and stared for a long time at the Preacher's face. He put a hand down to his father and smoothed his hair.

"You're gonna get that crown now, Daddy," Levi said, then backed up and shut the tailgate gently.

"He's dead, isn't he?" Benji asked his uncle.

Levi nodded and Benji hung his head low.

Levi turned and sat down on the bumper to fumble for a cigarette and lighter. He cupped his hand against the wind and snow and flicked the lighter over and over to snatch enough flame.

Jake returned from the woods and observed his son and his brother from a distance. There was something about his brother's reaction that tore at him. Maybe it was his nonchalance. The cavalier attitude toward their father. Sitting and smoking. No tears to be seen. No regrets. Levi appeared selfish, uncaring, in the face of the man that had kept them together when there was no one else to do so. Benji noticed his father first and traipsed toward him.

Jake ducked back through the fence and met his son.

"Grandpa's dead," Benji said.

"I know."

Levi looked back over his shoulder at both of them and took another drag of his cigarette. Jake pushed his son aside and went toward his brother.

"Guess we didn't make it," Levi said.

Jake grabbed his brother by his jacket, picked him off the bumper, and threw him into the snow. Levi fell in a heap, and Jake jumped on top of him with ferocity. He reared his fist back to hit his brother, and Benjamin grabbed his arm.

"No, Dad!" he exclaimed. "Stop!"

Jake shook his son away and hit Levi in the face. He wound up for another strike and then stopped. Levi looked up at his brother and Jake kept his fist ready. Levi appeared resolved to take it. He didn't fight.

Jake got off him, angry and disgusted, went to the driver's side, and got in. He was soaked from the snow and wiped his face and his tears with the back of his hand. He didn't care. He needed time to think, and he didn't want his brother or son to see him in this state.

Levi rolled over and groaned in pain. He grabbed at the bumper and Benji put his hands out to help. Levi used the side of the wagon and his nephew to straighten himself up and get to his feet.

"I'm sorry, Uncle Levi."

"Leave your daddy alone," Levi said to Benji, feeling his cheek. "I probably had it coming. Better to get it out than live with it. You get back in the wagon."

Levi spit blood on the ground and rested his hands on his knees. Benji took another glance through the icy window at his grandfather, then went back to his side of the car, opened the door, and got in. Levi leaned his way along the car before he opened his own door and got in. Together the three of them sat in silence and looked off up the mountain. The snow melted quickly on the hot hood and the wipers fought to flick the windshield clean.

"What do we do now?" Benji asked.

Minutes passed in silence, each with his own thoughts. The wipers became a timer and flicked back and forth, back and forth, back and forth. Jake looked at the gas needle and the temperature gauge, then turned the key to cut the ignition. The wipers stopped and the hum of the engine and the heater came to a calm. The wind and the snow quickly filled the void of noise.

"No way we could've made it from here," Jake offered. "Hasn't been a vehicle up there in who knows how long. And the place is hardly standing. I don't know. More fire. Arson. Time."

Levi reached into his pocket, pulled out his smokes, and offered one to Jake. He refused with a nod and Levi lit one for himself and cracked the window.

"Let's get on with it," Levi said.

"With what?" Jake replied. "There's nothing more to do. Dad's dead."

"No," Levi offered. "We finish the job. We at least get him up there. I didn't do all of this for nothing."

"He's right, Dad," Benji added. "Grandpa would want us to do that. He'd want us to finish the job."

Jake cleared the window frost with his sleeve and looked out the front at the falling snow.

"You can't carry shit," Jake finally said to his brother. "How do you expect we're going to get him up there? Can't get *you* up there."

Levi glanced at his brother.

"You just meet me outside."

UP THE MOUNTAIN

Jake pulled the heavy tailgate open and the three of them stared down at the Preacher. Levi closed the Preacher's eyes and Jake removed a familiar old handkerchief from his pocket. He put the handkerchief under his father's chin and tied it off at the top of his head, squeezing the old man's jaw closed. He then reached for the bible and tucked in it tight with his father and adjusted the blankets until they swaddled the Preacher tight.

Benji observed a process he'd never seen before. The brothers avoided looking at each other and focused only on the Preacher and the journey ahead. They strung ropes underneath the Preacher and pushed his body to different sides to cross and tie off. When they were finished, only the Preacher's face and boots were left to see.

Benji wiped away flakes that gathered on the exposed skin.

"I'm going to miss him," he said to his father.

"Me, too," Jake replied.

Jake put his arms under his father's shoulders, grabbed onto the ropes, and gently pulled him out and passed him to Levi. Levi took the ropes, Jake took the other end, and together they made their first steps to conquer the mountain.

The fence across the hidden road was the easiest point to cross, the narrowest point, and the only choice without barbed wire and other obstacles.

"We'll have to pass him over," Jake hollered over the wind to his brother. "How are we gonna do this?"

"I'll go through first," Levi replied. "You hand him over."

Jake didn't ask his brother if he could hold their father by himself. He expected him to. Levi pushed the fence apart and grimaced when he bent and stepped through. Jake passed the Preacher over the fence, and Levi used his back leg to steady himself and hold the old man. He cradled his father like a baby as the ropes dangled. Jake pulled at the wire, Benji crawled through the opening, and then it was Jake's turn. He bowed down and hugged the bottom wire and squeezed his way through.

Under the glimmer of gray sky, the brothers again took up the ropes and started the climb. Jake took the lead. The incline, the wind, and the snow fought against them. Their eyes watered from the blasts of air and the ropes stung in their frozen hands. The knee-deep branches poked from each side and the snow hid the rocks and the uneven terrain of the forgotten road. One rope over a shoulder, one foot ahead of the other. Every step shot hot pokers into Levi. It was up to him to match his brother in the lead and keep from dropping their package. There was no talking, no words spoken between them. They knew their job and kept moving. They could not stop. It was the last trip with the Preacher. Levi ignored the pain and let his thoughts run wild. Anything, anywhere else, any faces, any memories.

The sheets and the blankets flapped for freedom in the blowing wind and Benji ran between them to hold them down. The road disappeared in the buildup of snow and Jake led by memory of the place, using the tops of old wire fences and the scrubs of bushes that poked out along the sides as a guide.

Levi struggled as the pain throbbed for release, and he gritted his teeth and dug in with the crunch of snow under his feet. They slipped, stumbled, and fell, but kept on one foot at a time and kept their father from tumbling to the ground.

"You alright?" Jake stopped and called back to his brother.

"Yeah!" Levi hollered back, a lie.

"Keep moving!" Jake called again. "Almost there!"

Levi hummed a tune with his steps to get his mind off the pain. An old church tune they'd had to sing a thousand times. Many of them came naturally, burned into memory. His eyes were moist, his teeth chattered. The road was a foot deep with snow and the sun was veiled. Their feet froze until each step became a half a step and they made progress by inches.

The pain was intense for Levi. He'd done so much to escape the past and the unplanned consequences. No prayer or book or new experience would fill the emptiness he felt. Jake thought of life without his father and he swelled with emotion and guilt against the cold temperature. He remembered so many times gazing at his old man's hands wrapped around the steering wheel, the felt hat sitting perfectly on his head, the upturned corners of his father's mouth that always seemed to be there. He wondered what part of life had driven him to become an apostle to the unknown. Was it really the war, or something else, something unexplainable?

He was younger then, but Jake remembered the people from the mountain. The old farmers who paid cash on the barrelhead to have the Preacher come and speak at funerals. The teenage daughter pregnant and needing to be married as soon as possible. The man with the cancer who could not drive himself, so of course the Preacher volunteered to do it and left the boys to take care of each other.

He tried to think of his father as a young man. Going to war, losing a wife, and losing the land. Maybe preaching the gospel was something he couldn't lose. Maybe his faith had gotten him through losses that would've broken most men. Jake wished he had that kind of faith. It wasn't the Preacher's fault. Some things made little sense. He understood Levi more than he'd admit.

Each step took several seconds now until the road plateaued and gave way to a flattened area with ramshackle remains and an old church building bent with age and time. The brothers dropped to their knees and carefully slid their load to the ground. Benji stopped alongside them. The sun and the moon cast competing shadows across the gray wintery sky, and together they viewed the remains of the past all around them.

The burned-up land was now covered in new vegetation and snow, and the old church steeple still pointed skyward, though crippled to one side, and if the sky had been clear, they would've seen a great distance on most days to a dark river beyond. Over there was the scorched remnants of the old house, the porch slanted at an angle and filled in by time and nature. The walls were now made of vines and the roof had caved in long ago and piled high with snow.

It had been many years since the boys had come to this place. After the fire, time had taken its toll and the mountain was taking back the land. Maybe the Preacher knew, Jake thought to himself. The Preacher would see the Lord's hand in the return to nature, and he too wanted to be reclaimed, ashes to ashes, dust to dust.

Jake took a few steps from the body and stopped near an old water well and looked over at the dilapidated house. The front door was long gone, and he could see all the way to the back. He remembered his father as a young man walking the boys through the old house, and pointing to where he was born, and to the room where he and his three brothers slept.

Levi removed a bottle from his pocket and poured a swig of the warm liquor down his throat. He felt around for one more vial of morphine, but it was a wishful thought. A conjured escape. There was no more to be had.

Yet the journey was accomplished. Not as they envisioned. Not as they had planned. But it was done. Levi looked across at his brother. He observed his nephew and realized this was the boy's first time on the mountain. They'd brought a new member of the family up to lay the old man down. The Preacher would have been proud of this moment.

"Let's put him in the church," Levi called to his brother.

Jake peered at the steeple bent crooked by the winds and the roof warped and exposed by time, but he understood it and nodded his agreement.

They picked the Preacher up again and carried him to the porch.

"You got him?" Jake asked his brother, who nodded he did.

Jake pushed against the door with his shoulder until it gave. The door was still heavy with the age of old oak, and it scraped the floor as it went.

The building smelled of varnish and wet wood. Bits and pieces of jagged glass hung in the windows. They walked a step at a time down the aisle and carried their father. The wooden pews where the mountain folk used to sit were dirty with leaves blown in and piled up. Benji picked up a red-stained songbook blotched with mold that still hung at the back of each pew. The wooden pulpit stood front and center as if it waited for the return of the Preacher.

"Where should we put him?" Levi asked and swayed. "I need to sit down."

And this time, he dropped his end of the Preacher and collapsed. Jake placed the Preacher on the wood floor and joined Benji near his brother.

"Just need... to catch my breath," Levi said.

Jake pulled on Levi's jacket to look at the wound, weeping anew with fresh blood.

There was a sound from down the mountain. An engine and traction against the snow. Each of them heard it at the same time.

FALL OF AHAB

The sheriff missed the turn off the highway and skidded the Hulk to a halt. He threw it into reverse and the big tires bit into the road.

This was not how he'd planned to spend the holidays, though he felt more euphoric with each passing moment. He turned off the road and the big wheels churned the snow and the frozen earth. He gunned it with each turn of the wheel, over and over, until he came upon the wagon, abandoned and empty.

Hell.

He knew it. He'd tracked them down way too easily. His knowledge of the area, the connections he'd made through various associations, it had all paid off. Now, the inconveniences the little bastard put him through would also be paid for. He put the truck in gear and torqued the engine, climbed the hidden road, then smashed the fence down.

The headlights followed the impression of the road and churned through the snow. He felt carnal at the intensity swelling up inside of him. He was on the hunt, just like old times. *Cold, cold Korea.* Not only could he salvage the situation, but he'd bag a kill. It was good to feel so alive, so vigorous, and he hauled up the road as quick as the tires would take him.

The sound reverberated up the mountain and the brothers heard it. Jake grabbed Benji by the arm.

"Go on," said Levi, who struggled to his feet with all the energy he had left. "Get out of here. He'll try and take me back and that'll be the end of it."

Jake looked at his brother, caught between the safety of himself and his son, and that of his brother. Levi wasn't known for making the greatest of selfless decisions, yet the familial bond was still there.

"Who?" Jake asked.

"The sheriff," his brother answered with his remaining energy. "No time to discuss. Get Benji and go!"

Jake grabbed Benji and steered him out of the church. They tramped quickly into the woods and dropped behind a fallen log as the big truck roared up the top of the hidden road and pulled into the homestead. The sheriff brought the beast to a halt with Levi in the headlights on the church porch.

There he was, Levi Johnson, and the big shot raised a hand as if to wave at an old familiar face.

"Sonofabitch," the sheriff mouthed to himself.

Enough of this little bastard that upset his order. Levi broke the rules, *his* rules. He'd interrupted his holiday. He'd stolen from him. Levi Johnson was a mad dog. Levi Johnson was a criminal.

Levi Johnson would have to be put down.

The sheriff turned the truck off but kept the lights on. He stepped out and planted his heavy black boots into the snow. He reached in to grab the shotgun, then decided he didn't need it, and shut the door. He drew his revolver out instead and held it to the side. He looked around for signs of anyone else. He scanned the ground and saw several footprints.

"Where's your brother, Levi?"

"Nobody else here, Sheriff," Levi answered. "Just me and the Preacher."

The sheriff knew better and didn't like how exposed he was. He narrowed his eyes and looked for anything he could see through the falling snow and the gray, overcast day.

Levi noticed his father's bible on the ground. *Must've slipped out while we moved him,* he thought. He bent down toward his father's bible and put a hand to the ground to steady himself and to push back up. He shook the snow from it and wiped the cover. The sheriff brought the gun up and cranked back the trigger.

"You've got some things that belong to me," the sheriff told him.

Levi ignored the sheriff and thumbed through the bible. He slid an old photo from between two pages. It was Levi and Jacob at one of the Preacher's revival tent meetings. The Preacher stood between his sons with a hand on each shoulder.

"You better listen to me, boy!" yelled the sheriff.

Levi gazed at the picture. Innocent faces from a long-gone time. The quiet pride of the old man. Levi placed the picture back between the pages and continued to thumb through the book.

"Where's my money?" the sheriff asked.

Levi flipped through the pages at the many handwritten notes from the Preacher along the edges; notes to himself on verses, the birthdays of the boys and their mother, and dates of their travels and where he preached what lesson.

Levi continued to ignore the big man, which only incensed him further, so the sheriff cocked his revolver and fired a warning shot at Levi's feet.

The snow kicked up between his feet, but Levi barely flinched and peered up slowly at the sheriff. Benji tried to stand from their hiding place and Jake grabbed on to him and pushed him back down.

"Before you get too smart," the sheriff warned, his gun smoking in the cold air, "don't go thinking this is only about you. I don't get back what's mine, I'll take down everyone you ever knew. All of them. Relative, friend, won't matter. You can bet your sorry ass they'll be joining the Preacher."

The threat did not have the effect the sheriff expected, and Levi felt a rush of familial emotion he'd long forgotten. He smiled at the sheriff with a newfound defiance.

"Always the same with people like you," Levi said. "Get what you can. Get someone else to do the dirty work. You see, I've got this hole right here in my shoulder, and that comes from those boys you made a deal with. They didn't get the job done, Sheriff. You're gonna have to clean up your own mess this time."

The sheriff was unused to defiance. To see it and to hear it, it was too much. He wanted to kill Levi right then, immediately, but that would be short-sighted. There were still options.

"Where's the ledger?" the sheriff said. "Maybe we can come to an agreement. Set things right."

Levi shook his head. "I already know what kind of deals you make, Sheriff."

Then Levi smiled and added a bit more.

"But I tell you what, for old time's sake. You turn around and leave now, that ledger can stay lost."

Aah, this little bastard.

"Last warning," said the sheriff. "So help me God, you don't show me that ledger, I'm going to put you down right here, right now."

"He's gonna kill him, Daddy," whispered Benji.

"Stay here," Jake ordered Benji, then scurried from his hiding spot.

"Stop!" yelled Jake.

The sheriff's eyes darted toward the voice without moving his trigger hand, yet he didn't need to look. He knew who it was.

"That you, Jacob?" asked the sheriff.

Jake didn't answer and came closer into view until the sheriff saw him.

"Don't ruin your life over your brother, son," the sheriff said to him. "The Preacher knew he had one good boy. Used to tell me how thankful he was. How he didn't know what he'd do if you'd both gone bad. Your brother's got some things that belong to me. I get them back, I forget you were here."

It was a lie, but the sheriff hoped it would be enough.

"Don't want any trouble, Sheriff," Jake finally replied.

"Trouble is already here, Jacob. Your brother brought it, but you can walk right out of this. Let your brother stand on his own. What your daddy should've done a long time ago."

"Told you to stay out of this!" Levi called to his brother.

"A bit late for that," Jake replied.

The sheriff breathed a sigh. He was hoping for a clean ending, no loose threads. This would not be easy. Doable, but difficult.

"That's just like you," the sheriff called to Levi. "Getting your family involved. Making them pay for all your screw-ups."

"Came on my own accord, Sheriff," Jake replied, with his hands out low near his body. "If you want to take Levi back to jail, I'll stay out of the way. Needed his help to bring my father home. I've got no further use for him."

"Thanks," Levi said to his brother.

The sheriff clenched his jaw and moved his fingers. His experience and training had given him a strong intuition. His success depended on how much he controlled the situation. With both the brothers, he no longer had that control. They knew too much. They had the ledger. He could improvise but it was dangerous and messy. Better to retreat. Think of a different plan.

They think they can beat me.

Thirty years it had taken him to build things up, and now these sorry sonsofbitches were trying to take him down. He was back in the field now. Things had to be done. A good soldier did what was required. Action was everything. He couldn't walk away. Divide and conquer.

He turned his voice toward Jake.

"Let me finish this with Levi. You walk away clean. You were never here."

Jake paused to consider the offer, but there was no real thinking about it. He could never do it. He couldn't live with it. Besides, if everything his brother said about the sheriff was true, he couldn't trust the man, no matter the law or the badge.

"Can't do that, Sheriff," Jake replied.

The sheriff looked toward Jake. Now there was clarity. One shot, and then two, and then he'd figure out what to do about the money. Losing the money hurt, but the ledger was the real problem.

"If this is the end," Levi said, "something I want to confess to."

The sheriff didn't want to hear Levi Johnson anymore, not another word, but curiosity got the better of him and he continued to hold.

"There was this boy," Levi started. "Back in Vietnam. Big and dumb. Think his name was Buck."

The sheriff didn't know the name and didn't understand where Levi was going.

"This boy Buck wasn't the smartest. I mean, he was smart enough and all, but something not right. Something... *deranged*. But he was a helluva soldier. That's all they wanted. He seemed to sense things. Didn't matter where we were or where we were going. Shit would come down and Buck would be right there."

Levi coughed and cleared his throat to continue.

"Now, Buck. He enjoyed it. He liked being out there, hunting and killing those gooks. Taking their stuff. Taking... pieces of them. Little mementoes. And the other guys? They saw real quick. Stay away from Buck. He's dangerous. Not just to the enemy. To all of us."

Sheriff Price turned his head slightly and continued to listen.

"You see, most of us didn't want to be there. Just wanted to get home. It'd only take two months, maybe three, to know you wanted out of the shit. But not Buck. I mean, he *lived* for it."

Levi trailed off in thought before he picked back up.

"And then one night, we were somewhere we probably had no place being. Trying to keep quiet, do our patrol, get the hell out. And Buck did what

Buck does. We come upon a dead gook and Buck gets this smile across his face. You could see it no matter how dark it was. And he was cutting into that dead gook to get his trophy and I saw a gook coming up on him. A small man against big Buck. And the feeling I had? It surprised me, Sheriff. It really did. I figured those gooks were damn smart. They baited Buck. And they would've gotten him if I hadn't saved him."

"I saved that boy. And you know what he did? He tried to kill me. He didn't like that I saved him. Didn't like that I *knew* him. Knew what he really was."

"And that's when I learned, Sheriff. Some people just aren't worth saving. I think that's something my Daddy never learned. Buck tried to kill me… and I don't know if it was a… good versus evil thing, but I felt good when it was done. Buck was an evil piece of shit."

"You better get somewhere quick," the sheriff interrupted.

"When I saw that picture in your office," Levi continued, "the one with your boy in the sharp, pressed uniform and the cold, dead stare, he looked familiar."

Where's this little bastard going?

"Because the last time I saw your boy, the last time I saw Buck, I left him dead and rotting in the jungle."

The sheriff blinked. It was incredulous. *Could it be?*

The sheriff yelled and the blast hit Levi square in the chest and blew him off his feet.

"No!" shouted Jacob.

The sheriff wheeled quickly, nimbler than it would appear the big man could move. He put his aim toward Jake, but little brother was ready.

Two shots rang out and echoed across the mountain.

When the smoke cleared, the sheriff peered through the gray haze and snow and held his gun at the ready for another shot. He rarely missed, even if he couldn't see the entirety of his target. Then he felt something.

He stepped back and put a hand toward his chest. Something burned and grew in intensity. He looked down.

His girth had caught the bullet, and a stain grew near the hand on his chest. He staggered two more steps back and ripped at his jacket in shock at the pain. He'd been shot before, many years ago and a world away. The smell of burning flesh and melting ice and oily fires rose in his nostrils and he thought he heard voices. The enemy closing in.

"Ah," he muttered, "you little bastard. You little bastard!"

The sheriff felt a surge of pain, and he made a last gasp to recover. He came to life and swung his gun toward Jake. The second shot caused the sheriff's head to snap back, and his teeth clenched on his tongue. He collapsed to the cold ground and his hand released the gun and his mouth fell open. His eyes gazed off to one last place on the horizon.

Jake approached, his gun still raised and smoking against the cool air. Benji stood from his hiding place and ran toward his father.

"Stay back," Jake yelled to Benji, who stopped in his tracks.

Jake moved with caution toward the sheriff. He'd never shot a man before. He pointed his gun, ready to shoot again, but the sheriff had expired. Jake quickly went to his brother while Benji stepped closer to the sheriff. Frightened, he backed away and caught up to his father.

Jake bent down over his brother.

"Now, you messed it up," muttered Levi between spits of blood.

The emotions swelled inside Jake, and he looked at the gun in his hand and the blood around his brother. He tried to speak and couldn't. Benji bent down next to them.

"You know what to do," Levi forced out.

But did he? There were few choices left to keep himself out of prison, keep Benji out of the entire episode, and keep his brother alive.

"Give me the gun," Levi told him. "Put it… in my hand and pull the trigger."

Jake hated it. The decision burned in him. His brother was right. He didn't want to admit it, but this was the only way out.

"No, Dad!" Benji cried, fighting back tears. "We've got to help him!"

"I'm shot up, Benji," Levi told him.

The man and the boy looked at each other.

"Can't we do something?" Benji implored his uncle and father.

Levi coughed and a stream of blood percolated from his mouth. He closed and opened his eyes, then peered at Jake.

"I never… liked that song," Levi muttered.

"What song?" Jake asked. "What are you talking about?"

"Amazing… grace."

Levi's eyes grew enormous, then relaxed, and his head rolled to the side. His last bit of breath hit the cold air and evaporated. Jake lowered his head and Benji did the same. Thirty years of dreams and squabbles and hate and love and riding in backseats and the lights of county fairs and open bibles and songbooks and baptism and prayers, oh so many prayers, and sitting in hot, musty places and cold, creaky houses and waiting for treasures in heaven and thieves in the night.

"Uncle Levi!" Benji called, but there was no answer. Jake wiped his own tears away. There would be no long goodbyes.

Jake took the gun, put it in Levi's hands, and used Levi's fingers to fire it toward the sky. He carefully lay his brother's hand down, still wrapped around the gun. He went through his brother's pockets and pulled out his cigarettes, his lighter, and the remains of the bottle of whiskey. He rose and picked up the bible, dusted the snow off, and secured its contents.

It was the hardest work Jake had ever done. Benji followed his father inside and watched as Jake tucked the bible under his daddy's hands. They took one more look at the old man before shrouding his face with the sheet. Jake pulled out the bottle of whiskey and poured it across his father's wrappings, then took the knife and cut open the old pew cushions and pulled down some of the threaded drapes and piled up the bibles and songbooks around the Preacher and emptied the rest of the whiskey.

Jake lit a cigarette with one flick of the lighter and inhaled the smoke. He exhaled and remembered all the singing and the prayers and the old blind woman who used to sit up front in a pew just like this one, and old Mr. Simpson, who always had his handkerchief falling out of his back pocket.

He stepped back and took one last look, thought of one last memory, then tossed the cigarette in. Before long, the smoke rose black and thick, and the fires breathed on their own and licked up the rest of the curtains until they feasted on the walls.

Jake exited the old church with Benji close behind. The boy had aged years in minutes and his shock at events had turned to numbness. Everything he knew, the innocent child he was, disappeared with the flames and his grandfather.

They moved past Levi one more time, one last gaze on the brother and uncle. Jake went to the sheriff's body and grabbed the big man by the ankles and turned him toward Levi. With the sheriff's hat and gun kicked a few inches further afield, they left the Hulk with the keys in the ignition and the headlights on. If it was to look like a shootout, Jake reckoned things had to be arranged just right.

They observed the flames as they licked up under the steeple and cracked and smoked until they billowed out to take what the old forest fire had left behind. The smoke hung low across the top of the mountain and the sky appeared a swirl of darkness and gray as the fire joined heaven and earth together. A bolt of lightning cracked across the sky and struck the little church. Jake pulled Benji back and away from the scene.

Together, father and son traced their previous steps out. The fire cast light into the shadows of the woods, across the graveyard of memories and bones, and tendered guidance over their steps back down the mountain.

REVELATIONS

It was several months later, in another season, in a new year, when the temperature rose, and the snow gave way to afternoon showers. Spring had come earlier than usual and the jailbreak down in Boone gave way to events of the new year. Burns, the long-trusted deputy and guard on duty, was appointed the temporary sheriff until the case could be closed and a special election called. The singular pursuit that led to the demise of Sheriff Orville Price became lore and legend.

The official story was that Levi Johnson had overpowered Burns and made his escape. The ever-valiant Sheriff Price had chased him into the hills of Kentucky, only to lose his life in the line of duty. When the authorities inquired, Jake played dumb. He pretended anger at his brother for doing what he did. He thought his brother was taking the old man to a nursing home. With that, the narrative took hold and Boone fell into a new normal.

The days grew longer under the sun, and trips out to the bridge to fish with Benji were back in fashion. Jake felt the passing of his father and his brother. He'd not been to a church, not thought on religion for some time because of the memories it served up, but he planned to take Rachel, Benji, and the baby to a Sunday service for old time's sake. He recalled the potlucks with the buckets of chicken and candy baskets around Easter and the extra-large crowds that would come to pay a bonus for their weekend sins to a risen Jesus and then pray to turn over a new leaf before new temptations of summer arrived.

It was more reflection than he liked. It was hard to concentrate on his work or the family, or anything. He sat on the porch and thought of Levi driving up in the truck and parking by the shed and something else Levi had said, and what the sheriff had demanded.

Was it possible?

Jake bounded from his seat on the porch for the shed. The door had settled since it was last opened, and Jake used both hands to tug on the door and it scraped against the earth before it gave way. Light peeked in on the musty boxes of junk and books and tools and all kinds of things the old man had asked Jake to store when he retired from being a full-time preacher.

Jake reached a hand up to pull the string for the low hanging bulb. Now he could see all the stuff he'd shoved in it. The walls were lined with rusted buckets of paint, plumbing supplies, and pieces of furniture. The middle held the Preacher's boxes.

Jake went to the boxes, checked them for labels, and pulled a couple of flaps back before he stopped. This one was marked *communion* in his father's handwriting. He pulled back the flaps and opened it.

There were the Preacher's set of communion trays and the offering baskets made to look like crowns of thorns. He hadn't looked at them in years and he blew a sheen of dust from them.

When he looked down into the box, he saw something else and reached his hand in. He dragged the ledger out and opened the cover. He turned a few pages, and took a glance at the dates, and amounts of currency, and various codes. He read a series of letters and a repeat of "LJ" several times. He understood he was holding the secrets and misdeeds of the sheriff, and the final chapter of his brother's life. He closed it and set it aside, then brought the bag up and loosened the draw strings.

There was the cash; wads of bills of various denominations tied up and folded in rubber bands.

Jake shook his head and sat down on a box and looked out the opening of the shed. He gazed at the leftovers of life around him and shook his head again. How their lives had been so alike, and yet so different. Born of the same parents, they'd absorbed their experiences and pains and taken divergent paths. Then his shoulders shook. He looked around to ensure no one could see him, and he let the tears fall for all the lost time and the things left unsaid and undone and the bad luck. For the things that he would never understand about his brother and his father and would never have an answer for.

He put the money back in the bag, replaced the ledger on top, stacked the plates and baskets on top, then closed the box. He pulled the string to the bulb to extinguish the light and sat in the dark of the shed.

He wiped away the tears for the dreams of the Preacher who ministered to the lost souls of the South, and for the brothers who rode together in the back seat to help their daddy do it.

THE END

ABOUT THE AUTHOR

Daniel Parker is a teacher, a writer, and a public servant. He has a master's in urban planning and spent a year overseas in several countries. He lives with his wife and children in Tallahassee, Florida. This is his eighth book. Find more books by Daniel at http://bit.ly/DanielParker

Made in the USA
Columbia, SC
30 December 2021